Second Edition

THUNDER RIDES A BLACK HORSE

Second Edition

THUNDER
RIDES A BLACK HORSE

*Mescalero Apaches
and the Mythic Present*

Claire R. Farrer
California State University, Chico

Prospect Heights, Illinois

For information about this book, write or call:
    Waveland Press, Inc.
    P.O. Box 400
    Prospect Heights, Illinois 60070
    (847) 634-0081

To my Mescalero family—

"Lauren," "Harold," "Jay," "Delores,"
and "Nancy"

Contents

Acknowledgments

I owe an immense debt of gratitude to those on the Mescalero Apache Reservation who have made me feel welcome during the past thirty years and especially to Wendell Chino and the members of the Tribal Council who allowed me to work there. I especially acknowledge those to whom I am closest in my fictive family, whose pseudonyms appear in the dedication; they know who they are and what they mean to me.

My daughter, Suzanne, despite being uprooted from her home in Texas, learned to love the people and the land as much as did I. In fact, as we were leaving the reservation in 1975—and much to my chagrin—she found Apache people who were willing to adopt her formally, so that she would not have to return to Anglo civilization. I insisted she come back to Austin with me and then, in rapid succession, moved her to Washington, D.C., Santa Fe, New Mexico, and Urbana, Illinois. But a part of her also still considers the Mescalero Apache Indian Reservation home. Not only did she learn the language faster than I did, but also she and her Apache friends were and are never-ending sources of delight.

I am grateful to M. Jane Young who made excellent critical recommendations that improved the readability of the text. From her own work with Zuni people and long experience in the American Southwest, she helped improve the text of my Mescalero Apache work.

A special thanks to Apple, without whose Macintosh℠ (and its operating system that "speaks" English) I would still be writing paragraphs on different colors of paper and taking four times as long to finish anything.

Although I did not always take her advice, copy editor Wanda Giles saved me from my awkwardness and improved the text in general.

I am grateful to Thomas Curtin of Waveland Press who first suggested I do this book and then nurtured me through it as only a fine editor can. Without him, truly, the book never would have been written.

Second Edition Acknowledgments

Both Dr. Daniel E. Moerman of the University of Michigan, Dearborn, and his graduate assistant, Ms. Tina Palivos, have earned my gratitude for the excellence of their Study Guide and kind permission that allowed me to add a few queries of my own as well as to include it with this text, thus engendering the second edition. The guide they prepared addresses the questions most usually put to me by careful readers, whether in person, by telephone, or over the net (e-mail: cfarrer@oavax. csuchico.edu).

Finally, I am grateful to all those readers who took the time and effort to respond. Each author writes in a self-imposed vacuum; it is quite comforting to know someone out there not only reads but also reads critically what has been produced in a solitary study.

1

Time and the Mythic Present

Apache! The very word conjures visions of half-naked, tall, slender men with long, straight, black hair streaming in the wind behind them—hair held in place only with headbands that function as much to keep sweat from eyes as to confine stray locks—men whose sinewy legs caress the sides of sleek horses that have hooves virtually flying along the ground, raising occasional sparks as the units of horse and rider dart into and out of sight, disappearing into mountain vastness or the tall grasses of the plains. Hollywood and western novels have given us such visions of Apache men, ignoring the women or portraying them as only nubile maidens who are the objects of whitemen's lust and who are invariably chiefs' daughters. Perhaps there may be a few—a very few— Apache people who could step into the Hollywood and novelists' stereotypes and find the fit a comfortable one, but I do not know them; they are not among the more than 200 Apaches with whom I am well acquainted and who give the lie to the stereotypes.

Apaches, especially those of the Mescalero Apache Indian Reservation in southcentral New Mexico (Figure 1) and who are the ones I know the best, are like any other ethnic group of people: some are skinny and some chubby; some are short and some tall; there are good ones, some of whom are friends for life, and there are some on whom it is best not to turn one's back for their lying and backstabbing ways. In sum, they are like people everywhere. But they are different, too, as I have learned from my three decades of experience with the people of the Mescalero Apache Indian Reservation.

Contemporary reservations are in mainstream American culture. Sometimes they are of that culture as well, but not always. The reservations with which I am familiar, all in the Southwestern or Western states, have buckskin and Ultrasuede™; finely bred horses and 4 x 4 Broncos; TV, often with satellite dishes, and older relatives with the *real* stories; Teenage Mutant Ninja Turtles and Warrior Twins; California ranch-style houses and sweat houses; strollers and cradleboards; Wonder bread and fry bread. Reservation Indians attend to each other, to TV "stories," and to the people in narrative, whether those people are the stuff of what mainstream Americans call everyday life or label as legend, folklore, or mythology.

The Native American people on contemporary reservations live in concert with those who have gone before as they do with those who are here now; perhaps this is true for urban Indians, as well—I know few of them and do not feel qualified to comment. For the Indians I know on several reservations in the American West and Southwest, life is lived in what I term the "mythic present." What mainstream Americans consider to have happened long ago, if it happened at all, is real and present during everyday life on reservations. There is a co-presence of events in which the Warrior Twins engaged and those taking place around a dinner table; this is the mythic present. Both the Long Ago and the Now are present together in thought, song, narrative, everyday life, and certainly in religious and ritual life.

The mythic present includes those who have gone before and who are remembered today. Sometimes they are culture heroes and heroines; sometimes they are tricksters, like the irascible Coyote, who has frailties as do all people but who, like each of Creator's children, also has worthy attributes. Regardless of who they are, the reality of those from the mythic present is as tangible to most Indian people as is that of the person sitting next to you at the ceremonial or the baby you

Figure 1. The Mescalero Apache Indian Reservation, established in 1873 by executive order of President Grant, today encompasses about 720 square miles in southcentral New Mexico. (Map courtesy of the University of New Mexico Press.)

tuck into bed at night, or your spouse or lover. It is the oscillating movement between the mythic present and the lived present, as I call what we perceive as reality, that gives contemporary Indian reservations their special character, their sense of depth, their roots, their rationale and exemplar. And it is the mythic present in concert with the lived present that are my concerns in this book.

Everything in the following chapters is true. However, I have taken some liberties. Time has been collapsed; things that happened in 1978, for example, have been merged with those that occurred in 1985, or 1988, or any of the other years between 1964 and the present—the times I have spent on the Mescalero Apache Indian Reservation. So, while all that is in the following chapters did actually happen, the events may have been separated by several years of real time.

The "ethnographic present" is the term that anthropologists use for such a collapsing of time. All events are related in the present tense, even when they happened some time ago. The ethnographic present is also the mode of discourse that Indians themselves use when speaking of events from myth or the long ago. It is as though those events were happening in concert with the events in which people who are alive today participate. This commingling of long-ago time, place, character, and activity with the present constitutes the mythic present. Thus, time has a different character, a different dimension, on Indian reservations than it does in mainstream American life.

Time is a concept that we all take for granted, without realizing that it is an artificial construct. Mainstream American ideas of time consisting of sixty-minute hours, with each minute having sixty seconds, can be traced to intellectual achievements of ancient Babylonians, people who lived—millennia before Christ's birth—in what is now Iraq.

Similarly, our Western idea that each month consists of four weeks, each with seven days, is also an artificial construct, as a glance at any calendar makes clear with some months having thirty days, some thirty-one, and one either twenty-eight or twenty-nine.[1]

Mescalero Apache people are fully aware of the mainstream American clock and calendar times and, indeed, function by them in much of their daily lives. However, they also have their own "Indian time." Indian time is not precisely linked to Anglo time.[2] The business of time, when considered cross-culturally, can be very confusing.

Often Anglos complain because things "don't happen on time" on Indian reservations. They most certainly do happen on time; it is just that "on time" takes on different connotations in the two separate cultures. Indian time, as it is called by Native people themselves, is governed by participants rather than a clock; it is when things and participants are all present and ready. That time may be ahead of or behind clock time. Edward T. Hall (1967, 1969, 1977, 1983) has discussed this issue of time in several books. His terms "polychronic time" (several things occurring at the same time) and "monochronic time" (when one thing happens at a time in sequence) are useful. Native American people operate on polychronic time; when all the swirl of preparatory activities coalesce with the necessary participants and ingredients, the event occurs. Obviously, one cannot have a dance if the dancers are not present or if the musicians are not ready. So, on most Indian reservations, saying a dance begins at 8:00 P.M. is to say that sometime after dinner, when the musicians are ready and when the stage is set and when the dancers are present, we will dance: this is a typically polychronic attitude. An astute observer might well see some of the preparations as they occur—perhaps musicians tightening drumheads, or a person going from camp to camp to announce that the dancers are painted—and, through such observations, realize that the dance is not yet quite ready. But Anglos, being firmly ensconced in monochronic time, have a tendency to ignore the polychronic events and to consider the dancing as being forty-five minutes late when the first dancer does not appear until 8:45. Anglos are equally appalled when they arrive promptly at eight only to find that the dancing has been going on for half an hour or more. Time is indeed perplexing when one is operating in a cross-cultural context, as Anglos or other non-Indians are when on Indian reservations or as reservation Indians are when operating in mainstream American culture.

People's names can also be a problem area between mainstream Americans and reservation Indians. Most Mescalero Apache people do not like to have their names mentioned in books. Some of the people I write about did give permission for their actual names to be used, but others did not. Therefore, almost all of the names in this book are pseudonyms. But they represent very real people, some of whom are or were well-known off the Reservation.

For example, Wendell Chino is the real name of the president of the Mescalero Apache Tribe. Through the more than twenty-five years of his tenure as tribal president, there have been many successful law cases brought under his name and that of the Tribe as a corporate entity; his name can be found in law books and often in newspaper articles.

And Bernard (BERN-ard; rhymes with Leonard) Second, whose name appears often in the chapters that follow, was a real person and was the man from whom I learned much of what I understand about Mescalero Apache people. He died in 1988, still a young man, and I miss him—especially as I write this book—for it was he who was responsible for my family connections at Mescalero. Bernard was active in the National Indian Youth Council and in various ecumenical councils; he was the narrator for films and television programs on his people or, on one occasion, on Central American people. He was highly regarded among Native Americans. He lives still in my memory, as I trust he will for you in the other chapters of this book.

The two well-known names of Chino and Second are used here, as are those of my daughter and myself; but no other real names are used, even when people gave permission me to do so. People deserve their privacy. Being an anthropologist is intrusive enough without also subjecting the people to possibly unwanted attentions from strangers.[3]

The purpose of this book is to allow non-Indians some insight into what it is like to live on a contemporary Indian reservation. There are moments of joy and incredible beauty, just as there are moments of sorrow and horridness; in these aspects, life on a reservation is like life anywhere in the United States—or anywhere else in the world. Yet there are some differences that can be difficult to comprehend.

Most Native North American[4] people live simultaneously in two cultures: their own, Native one and the one of the larger, mainstream American society. They are enriched by having two traditions upon which to draw while also being impoverished by sometimes feeling they are not fully accepted into either one.

Many non-Indian Americans feel the same way when they have strong family or ethnic traditions; this is especially true of first- and second-generation immigrants to this country, as can be seen today among Hmong or Mien people who want to learn quickly to become proper Americans while still feeling that particular aspects of their own home culture are important. Often people cling to the old culture's festivals, ceremonies, food, and items of belief; these become valued markers of ethnic identification to help define who, for example, is Hmong-American and who is not.

Native American people have similar pulls on their loyalties and beliefs. In some ways theirs is an easier problem in that there are reservations. When one lives on a reservation, the vast majority of other residents are also of one's own tribe who know, even if not all believe in and follow, the same traditions and who share the same history. Members of each household on the reservation will feature the same foods prepared in similar ways for particular occasions. Just about everyone on a reservation has heard the same stories, even if they are told in slightly different ways. Everyone knows the same rules for politeness and decorum, who can marry whom and why, who is forbidden to marry whom and why, and how the world came into being. All of these things, and others as well, make ethnic identity easier to define when people live on reservations.

But reservations can as easily be perceived as prisons. Reservations have boundaries that often seem more permeable for outsiders than for the Indians themselves. Reservations are places where the United States government and its agents are a daily presence. Often job opportunities are limited on reservations, and there is depressing poverty. Many reservations are the shrunken enclaves that remain after treaties were broken and land, once promised, has been confiscated by the U.S. government. Customs learned on the reservations often differ from those of mainstream Americans, making Native people feel out of place and the object of curiosity when they are off-reservation. Most Native people I know view reservations as a mixed blessing while adamantly maintaining their aboriginal rights to more land than they have.

And not all Native Americans live on reservations. That is important to keep in mind. I write of reservation Mescalero Apaches; yet, there are many Mescalero people who live in other parts of the United States, in Mexico, or in other foreign countries. What they all share in common is the sense that the reservation is home, even if they have had little life experience there.

It is also vitally important to bear in mind that I am not an Indian. I am an outsider, albeit one with a great deal of time and experience on the Mescalero Apache Indian Reservation. No one like me, an anthropologist-folklorist—or journalists or historians or any non-Indians—can ever truly represent what it is to be an Indian, to be a Native American and live as a minority in what was once a land populated only by other natives. Nonetheless, through the graciousness of friends and fictive[5] family, I have been privileged to share everyday life, both the mythic present and the lived present, with several generations of people from the Mescalero Apache Reservation. My perceptions are just that, mine. They have validation from some Apaches and are denied by others. My view is that of an informed visitor, and that is also my goal for readers: to provide an informed visitor's perspective, whether a reader visits the Reservation in person someday or knows it only through the pages of this book.

My first visit was in 1961 when, newly arrived in the Southwest, my former husband and I drove through the reservation land. The Mescalero Apache Indian Reservation is a particularly beautiful place. Most of it is mountainous and remains green all year round, although in some summers fires are a problem. The mountains are steep sided and are cross-cut by narrow canyons. For reasons of terrain, people often refer to directions as "up" (a mountain), "down" (a mountain), or "across" (a canyon). There is only one major road, Highway 70, an east-west federal road that recently was widened to four lanes through the entirety of the Reservation. Highway 24 between Mescalero and the community of Cloudcroft has only two lanes, as does the road linking the Inn of The Mountain Gods on the reservation with central Ruidoso. Highways 70 and 24 are open to tourists, but numerous narrower roads are not.

Many of the living areas are visible from Highway 70, but others are hidden away on those narrow roads. Most houses are set into the terrain with as little modification of the land as is possible. Lawns are rare, and generally considered unnecessary. Most people keep the areas around their homes immaculately clean. Still they sometimes seem cluttered with corrals (horses are still important, although almost everyone relies on pickup trucks or cars), sometimes sheds for tack and hay, vehicles, tipi poles (for summer encampments or to be used when houses overflow and it becomes necessary to erect a "guest house"—a tipi), and often a camper shell. Despite these additions, the general impression is of a series of clean and tidy mini-communities meandering up the sides of mountains.

I did not become acquainted with people of the Mescalero

Reservation until 1964, the date of my first fieldwork. Visits were aperiodic and of very brief duration between 1964 and 1971, when our family left Alamogordo, New Mexico, close to the Mescalero Apache Indian Reservation, for San Antonio, Texas, a long day's drive away from both Alamogordo and Mescalero. While living in San Antonio, I entered graduate school at the University of Texas in Austin.

Serendipity and some conscious decisions led to my choosing the Mescalero Apache Indians as my fieldwork population for dissertation research in anthropology and folklore a few years later. By the time I was ready to do fieldwork, I had been divorced; my then twelve-year-old daughter, Suzanne, and I went to live at Mescalero in September of 1974 for an academic year of research, staying through early September of 1975. Our moving there had been preceded by a year and a half's worth of negotiation between me and Wendell Chino who, as president of the Mescalero Apache Tribe and Tribal Council, acted on behalf of the entire Council and Tribe. Wendell and I forged an agreement whereby I could gather dissertation data in exchange for providing the Tribe with educational liaison services (gleaned from my time as a classroom teacher and as a graduate student) and in exchange for my preparing curriculum materials stressing Apachean themes for the children in the reservation grammar school.

Between 1976 and 1988, I visited the Reservation each year for varying periods of time. In some years I stayed for only a few days, and in other years I stayed much longer. I almost always was there for the major religious and ritual event, the public girls' puberty ceremony that takes place each July. This is a time of homecoming, not just for members of the Mescalero Apache Tribe but also for their friends and those Anglos who used to live on the reservation whether they were school teachers, Bureau of Indian Affairs (BIA) employees, other government employees, tribal employees, those attached to the Indian Health Service (IHS) hospital on the Reservation as health care professionals, or even anthropologists-folklorists. On these return visits, I rarely stayed in motels; usually, I stayed with a fictive family member, most often in Bernard's house.

In November of 1988 Bernard Second died. He had been gutą́ą́ł/singer (a ritual specialist and holy man)[6] for the

Mescalero Apache Tribe as well as my primary consultant and fictive brother from 1975 until his death. Bernard's family became our fictive family as our family become fictive relatives to them; for example, Bernard called my mother "Mom" while she always affectionately referred to him as "that dear boy," much to his amusement. The fictive family relationships continue through to the present, even though Bernard, who initiated them, has died.

Always finding excuses that kept me from facing the pain of losing one to whom I'd been so close for so long, after Bernard's funeral I did not return to the Reservation until the summer of 1991, two and one-half years after his death. Other fictive family members and friends kept in touch nonetheless and, finally, in June 1991 I returned to photograph a private

Bernard Second and the author in August 1975. Note the tape recorder on the tree limb and that Farrer is taking notes, while both she and Second are in rather formal poses. (Michael Barnes photo.)

Farrer and Second in July of 1983. Note that Second is writing Farrer's field notes for her, and that the previously formal scene is now an informal one inside a tipi. Ethnographers often find that long-term fieldwork involves many changes of roles. Also note the rolled up portion of the tipi cover; this, combined with movement of the tipi flaps, allows what is jokingly called "Indian air conditioning." (Adrienne S. Harmon photo.)

puberty ceremonial for the parents of the girl who was being honored, a service I often provide. It was a difficult time for me, for one of Bernard's primary responsibilities had been the singing of girls' puberty ceremonials.

The girls' puberty ceremonial is vitally important for the Mescalero Apache people, and that four-day, four-night event forms the structure of this book.

Each year around the Fourth of July holiday, the Tribe as a whole stops to celebrate the attainment of womanhood by its girls. In a matrilineal society, where kinship and descent are traced through one's mother, it is truly joyous to have new young women who will become the future mothers of the tribe. In July, the ceremonial lasts for four days and four nights, in the manner described in the following chapters. Some parents or guardians of girls-women who have reached initial menses (and therefore, by definition, *are* women) choose to have a private ceremonial rather than the public one. Private ceremonials may be only a day long, but the majority of them are held for two days. In increasing numbers of families lately, private ceremonies are also being performed for the full four days.

A ceremonial is a very expensive affair, for which families prepare literally for years. Through the three decades that I have been going to or living at Mescalero, I have witnessed, and often photographed, dozens of puberty ceremonials as a portion of the fieldwork that has allowed me to come to know the Apache people of the Mescalero Reservation.

Fieldwork in anthropology usually lasts for a year or so. Some anthropologists do far less and some, like me, do far more. When it becomes long term, as it has in my case, it becomes very complicated. As I have said elsewhere (Farrer 1991), one's fictive family is no less loved for not having been born into it. The relationships, rights, and obligations that build over the years are honored through, and beyond, death. So the anthropologist-folklorist becomes a person of two cultures as well, sometimes feeling fully at home in neither of them. I often miss the Reservation and long to see fictive relatives and friends; but, when I am there, there are always things that are closed to me, because I am not truly one of ^{n}dé/The People, the Apaches. I am an outsider. Yet, I am privy to things that other outsiders do not see or about which they do not know. If there is such a thing as an "outside insider," it characterizes many anthropologists and folklorists who do long-term fieldwork with one group of people. Living such a life can be as difficult as living as an Indian person in an Anglo world.

Nonetheless, at the heart of it, I am an outsider. But perhaps that kind of distance is what is needed for those who have never experienced reservation life to learn just what it is like to live on an Indian reservation in today's world, what it is like to live in the mythic present.

In the pages that follow, I present a composite of the dozens of ceremonials I have attended. The setting is the present, for the same things described in the following chapters can be seen now—with the exception of Bernard singing the ceremony. The girl I call "Stephanie" really exists and she is, as described, a descendant of Geronimo; I really did photograph her ceremonial in the mid-1980s. The photographs of a ceremonial girl that are in this book are not of her. As with the mythic present, specific events that actually occurred in one particular time have been moved about a bit in order to present a word picture of both a ceremonial and the mythic present in concert with the lived present.

Notes

[1] Just exactly what is a month? People can easily observe two different lunar cycles (Williamson 1987:43–47; Williamson and Farrer 1992:12–15). A synodic cycle, or a synodic month, is that time from a new moon (when there is no moon in the sky) through each of the moon's phases and back to a new moon again; it takes 29.530588 days: 29 days, 12 hours, 44 minutes, 2.9 seconds. There is also a sidereal month of 27.3217 days, the length of time it takes the moon to reappear in the same relative position to a given star. Obviously, what we in mainstream American society commonly call a month relates precisely to none of these cycles and is a highly artificial construct, as are other common structurings of time.

[2] "Anglo" is a term used in the Southwestern United States by Indians and non-Indians alike. It means non-Indian, non-Hispanic, non-African-American. Most Southwestern people find it a preferable term to whiteman, or any other designation.

[3] Paradoxically, some people are upset that their names are not used here. Knowledge at Mescalero is usually owned by individuals, in contrast to the free access to knowledge that mainstream Americans insist is the norm. So the use of knowledge that came to me from a particular person should be acknowledged. Still I fear hordes of people descending upon Mescalero, looking for a specific person or family, demanding information that is not normally shared with just anyone who happens to be curious and who wanders by. This protective attitude of mine, in regard to safeguarding names even of those who said I had permission to use theirs, is probably a remnant from the 1960s when I saw so-called hippies seeking truth from any Indian person encountered. Although I miss much of the joy and love of the hippie co-culture, it was not necessarily a pleasant time for reservation Indians, and I choose not to be responsible for even a small repeat of that scenario—a real threat, since the July ceremonial is listed on many tourist must-do promotions.

In order to pay (an appropriate practice at Mescalero) for the knowledge of my limited understanding, I participate in exchanges—usually of goods or services (such as photographic services) or very rarely of money. Since this book concerns people of the Mescalero Reservation in general, as well as my fictive family in particular, half of my profits from its sale go directly from the publisher to the Mescalero Apache Tribe; this is also in accordance with a portion of the agreement Wendell Chino and I made in 1974.

4 "Native American" as a term is technically more accurate than "Indian," since Columbus was wrong in his attribution of the native peoples he encountered as being a part of the Indian subcontinent. I use the two terms interchangeably, as, indeed, do most Native people I know.

5 "Fictive kin" or "fictive family" are terms anthropologists use to describe "as if" relationships. My fictive family at Mescalero treats me *as if* I were a sister in the family. In fictive kin relationships there are no consanguineal (with the blood) ties and no formal affinal ones (affixed, as when one receives in-laws as kin through their being affixed to one through a marriage.)

Fictive relationships differ from adoptions. When a person is adopted into a family, that person is *legally* considered to be a family member. When a person becomes a fictive relative, everyone agrees to abide by social conventions wherein the person is treated in the same way as would be someone born into the family; however—and it is a very big caveat—there are no jural (i.e., legal) claims the person can make, nor is there any basis in either Anglo or traditional law for the person's actually being a part of the family.

Nonetheless, the fictive relationship is one that can be fraught with emotion and caring. Children born into my fictive Mescalero family, or in-marrying spouses, are introduced to me as "shimá/mama," "auntie," or "sister," as is appropriate for the newest family member.

6 Whenever an Apache word appears for the first time, it is immediately followed by its gloss, or translation, with a diagonal slash separating the Apache from the English.

Apache words are formed with different phonemes (sounds that are meaningful in the language) than are English words. Apache vowels may be high tone (indicated with a short diagonal line over the vowel, á) or low tone (no indication); they may also be rising or falling, neither of which is indicated here. Vowels may also be nasalized (indicated with an inverted comma under the vowel, ą) or they may have both high tone and nasalization (indicated with both marks, ą́). Finally, long vowels are indicated by a doubling of the vowel (such as, aa). Consonants are also somewhat different. There is a syllabic n (indicated by ⁿ, since it also carries high tone) and a glottal stop (indicated by a question mark without the period: ʔ). In addition to consonant combinations not common in English (such as tl or dl), there is also a fricative l (indicated by ł or Ł).

2

Arriving

No matter from which direction I approach the Mescalero Apache Indian Reservation, I go from relatively low lands (although they are all above 3,000 feet) into high mountains. And no matter how many times I drive in, whatever the weather, I have an uncontrollable urge to open the windows of the car. I judge how far I am from my destination by the smell of the forest. In the last three decades that I have been making the trip, I have been surprised that my thoroughly Anglo nose has learned to smell Apache style.

The smell is of pine and oak and piñon and juniper; of old leaves and new buds; of wood smoke with a tinge of horse; of old memories informing new lives. It is a smell that is alive and is particularly acute if it has been raining—or is still raining; then the smell incorporates whiffs of saturated ground or wisps of dusty dryness being relieved.

I drive past the hidden caves where ancestors of today's people hid from the United States Army or where they lodged in times before even that—these smells are of poignant times and things better left untouched.

The drive always also brings a narrative of creation time to mind. Bernard told me many versions of how the world came into being. Those versions all shared certain features.

In the Apachean conception of creation, Creator took four days to provide people with the world that we know. First came the separation of Sky and Earth with the appearance of Light and Water, as well as other natural phenomena. Next, on the second day, came the plants and tiny animals. On the third day, Creator made what Bernard always referred to as the "four-leggeds," the larger animals. Finally, on the fourth day of creation, Creator made people—specifically the Apache people. Rather than being the epitome of creation, as in the biblical Genesis, people are the weakest link in the entire chain of being, for we require all that preceded us in creation in order to live.

Oftentimes as I enter the Reservation, I see deer or elk. They, too, remind me of the beginningtime when creation occurred. It is said that at that time people and animals could talk to each other. To this day, animals are thought of in kin terms and are known to be coequal with people. So, when a hunter must take the life of an animal to provide meat for a family, a prayer is always addressed to the spirit of the animal; the prayer explains that the animal must die for the people to live. The belief is that, if the animal is addressed properly and respectfully, the animal's spirit will communicate with the other animal spirits and they will be willing to be reborn. Should a hunter fail in his duty to the animals, they will withhold themselves from him, and his family will suffer for his arrogance in thinking that he was somehow better than the four-leggeds.

Plants, too, capture my attention as I note a yucca that has leaves used in making baskets and that sends up an edible stalk with edible white flowers. Or I note that chokecherries are almost ready to pick and enjoy. Or I see "Indian bananas," the pickle-shaped pods of another cactus that, when ripe, taste remarkably like tropical bananas. Sometimes I note the mesquite trees and think how many in the southwestern United States think of mesquites as being trash trees that clutter up, are messy, and take a lot of water. But they also produce great quantities of fruit in pods that can be eaten when green or when dry. The drier they become, the sweeter they are. And I smile when I see the piñon trees, for I always think of children looking like chipmunks in the early fall when the piñon nuts ripen. A child in the southwest quickly learns to put a bunch of piñon nuts into one side of the mouth and use

Mescalero Apache Indian Reservation land is primarily moun-tainous. Sierra Blanca Peak, the snow-capped mountain, is over 12,000 feet in elevation. On the back (north) side of the mountain, there is a tribally owned and operated ski area: Ski Apache. (Claire R. Farrer photo.)

the tongue to transfer a nut to the front, where it is then cracked open with the central or lateral incisors; next the tongue extracts the nut meat while the shell is spat out: it is really an elegant maneuver. The smell of fall, with its fragrance of piñons, is always a favorite of mine.

As I approach my destination, a house belonging to my fictive family or to good friends, the smell takes on a measure of seasonality: perhaps the crackling crispness of winter's dry cold; or the soft warmth of summer that seems to seep into one's pores; or fall's seductive sunniness that has just a hint of an edge to it; or maybe the new-plant smell of spring.

Sometimes the smells begin to tell me that people are home and cooking or, all too often, that someone has recently died and I wonder if I, too, will soon be crying over the loneliness I will feel if it is someone I have known and loved through the years.

These smells and their information are not magical or

Major roads into the Mescalero Apache Indian Reservation have signs posted to alert visitors they are on reservation land and to direct them to the center where tourist information may be secured. (Claire R. Farrer photo.)

mystical. They are simply the result of living in touch with oneself and one's surroundings. They are the result of business the people of the Mescalero Apache Indian Reservation take very seriously, indeed: the business of living in harmony and balance so that all in one's surroundings speak—perhaps not with the voice of a human, but understandably nonetheless.

My excitement at returning once again to what seems like my second home is always communicated to my traveling companion. In the old days it was my daughter, Suzanne (now grown and no longer the de facto anthropologist and folklorist), and our dog, a miniature poodle named Cinnamon for her color. Now the communication is with Nełįįyé/burden bearer (in old Apache) or /dog (today's more common gloss). Nełįįyé is most often called Nellie, because Apache phonemes are so difficult for most English speakers to pronounce. Some people at Mescalero say Nellie should really be called dibéhé/sheep, for she is a white, standard poodle—about the size, shape, and appearance of a slim sheep and every bit as woolly.

It is easy to understand why Apache friends are amused at the sight of us: think of a woman looking like a female Indiana Jones in costume and baggage, complete with hat— against the strong Southwestern sunshine—but with notebook, pen, camera, tape recorder, and tapes instead of a whip, working on an Indian reservation with an uptown dog whose coiffure is always impeccable while the anthropologist's is rather haphazard. Even I laugh when I see pictures of myself on the reservation. Now think about the kinds of comments that flow when Apache people remind me that the miniature poodle, Cinnamon, was that color at a time when my own hair was reddish-brown and I was slim and that Nellie, the standard poodle, is large and white while my hair is now gray and my body has taken on grandmotherly countours. Color coordination and bodily contour taken to their n^{th} degree, as I apparently have done, are highly amusing to my Apachean friends.

Color, almost as much as smell, tells me I am at Mescalero once again. Sometimes it is the jumble of colors of a summer ceremonial: bright paint colors of cars and pickup trucks on the ceremonial mesa; the blue-green of the evergreen trees; the sapphire blue of New Mexican skies; the white of thunderheads that build up in the summertime over the mountains; the bright brown eyes of the children as they successfully beg for just one more hot-pink cotton candy cone; or maybe the blue going to gray and burnt umber to black of an approaching summerstorm.

People of the deserts know when it is going to rain. They know even before the high, fluffy thunderheads stack themselves up against the mountains in the afternoon. They know even before the sun is clouded over and the temperature drops. They can smell rain when the humidity begins to rise and is not even perceptible to those from climates where rain is abundant. Desert people can feel their skin's pores stretching to absorb each drop that may fall on them. Hours before there is any visible sign, they know—through body knowledge—that rain will fall this day.

Rain: all depends upon rain. And it is so elusive in the high deserts and encircling mountains. It comes only during the summer monsoon season and then it is notoriously unreliable, quite literally falling upon the front of one's house but not in the back yard or raining on one part of a meadow while the rest bakes and threatens to crack open from the lack of water.

Rain brings mud on those roads on the Reservation that are not yet paved. Once when my little car sunk up to its axles in mud, appropriately enough in Mudd Canyon, I was taking a child home. At her insistence, I had been teaching her to read and write in "Indian," as most Mescaleros informally term their language. Friends, who literally lifted the car out of the mud on that occasion as well as other similar ones, had been partially responsible for my buying a four-wheel-drive vehicle, for, as they noted, we were all getting older, and they were not at all sure their backs would hold out for many more years with the seemingly incessant lifting of my cars out of the mud it seems I cannot avoid.

Thinking about mud, and in low four-wheel drive, I gracefully slid to a stop in the midst of a big puddle and barking, jumping dogs. Just about everyone at Mescalero has a dog or four. If you are newly visiting or if it has been a while since you have been at a particular home, it is always a good idea to honk your horn to get the attention of folks inside the house, then open a slit in your driver's side window, just enough to inquire whether or not these are biting animals before opening your door and risking your body. But even before I could open the window, my youngest daughter-niece,[1] Nancy, was on the porch shooing dogs and simultaneously yelling, "She's here! Shimá/mama, it's Auntie! She's here."

Amidst hugs and mud and yipping dogs, I gratefully entered the house, shedding muddy shoes and wet sweater, where Lauren, the youngest sister in my fictive family, was pouring coffee and indicating, by pointing with lower lip and chin, the steaming plate of fry bread next to the bowl of deer meat chili stew she had freshly prepared for my arrival. "Sit. Eat. It's been a long drive. Nancy, close that door and get off your Auntie. She'll be here a while. Let her eat now."

As I ate, Lauren told me of an old lady who had befriended me several years before who was now in a nursing home. "Betty, that one like The-Three-Who-Went-Together, that one is now in Roswell. They say she is like a child now and can't remember even her own kids. She thinks she's living back in that camp where the three of them lived, up beyond Elk and Whitetail. I guess that happens to old people sometimes."

Between mouthsful of fry bread, I asked, "Alzheimer's?"

"Au/yes. That's what they said. It just hurts the family so, when she doesn't know them anymore. And she had a lot of kids and grandkids. She don't remember one.''

Munching the fry bread and savoring the strong, sweet coffee, I was again reminded of the economy afforded conversations by the mythic present. Yes, Betty had lived like The-Three-Who-Went-Together, for Betty was a co-wife in a sororal polygynous family. She and her sister had shared a husband, in the old Apache way. Not every man had a polygynous household and, when one did, it was considered to be a better arrangement when the women were sisters; having grown up together, it was assumed that sisters already knew how to get along with one another and to share. And, after all, it is their family for whom they are raising the children anyway. Just as Lauren's children call me shimá, in Apache, because Lauren and I treat each other as blood sisters do, Betty's children and those of her sister considered both women to be their mothers. But none of this had to be said overtly. It is sufficient to say, "that one like The-Three-Who-Went-Together.''

The grandparents tell of a time, a very long time ago, shortly after the people had joined together as ^{n}dé, when two sisters fell in love with the same man. Nor could he choose between them, for the strengths of one balanced the weaknesses of the other. Each woman was beautiful and industrious. Each was also a proper person who would not allow her own happiness to interfere with the happiness of another and most assuredly neither would hurt another. So, after long consideration, the two sisters suggested that the man marry both of them. Then no one would have to choose, and each would be happy.

The man, who was an excellent hunter and provider, thought long and carefully. By marrying two sisters, he was also taking on the additional responsibility for providing for all of the children they would have plus the meat and service debts he would owe the parents of his wives. Not only would he have two families himself plus that of his wives' parents, but also he would retain responsibilities in his own matrilineage, to his own sisters and their children. It was a formidable task he was contemplating, a task that would last all of his life. Yet, it was a task he accepted with grace and dedication.

The three of them married and became the kind of family each person wishes to have: when one had, all had; when one laughed, all laughed; when one was sad, all were sad; when one rejoiced, all rejoiced. They shared not only among themselves, but also among the band as a whole. And it seemed that the more they shared, the more they had to share. Everyone enjoyed being with them and having them in the camp as members of the band.

And when all the ^{n}dé gathered together, as they sometimes did, especially for girls' puberty ceremonies at the time in the summer when the sun stands still, the family of the man with two wives (or, as some said, the family of the two women with one husband) was the family at the center of attention. As all of us do, the three of them grew older. They were grandparents and then their grandchildren had children. Their hair turned gray and then pure white. The fat under their skin gradually disappeared until their skin became like the thinnest hide—more like processed gut than hide—since one could almost see through it to their very bones. They walked slowly and others had to move their camp for them when ^{n}dé moved on, always moving southward toward the place foretold in the prophecies.

And then, one summer morning, he could not rise from his bed. His wives brought him the most nourishing soup. They lavished care on him as they had all their adult lives. And, when they were out of his hearing, they wept, for they knew that soon his spirit would leave his body and for the first time in over fifty winters they would not be the-three-who-traveled-together.

But their sorrow was for nothing. Creator, hearing their muffled sobs, came to them—all three of them—one night in a dream they shared. Creator reminded them of their earlier unselfishness, of their willingness to share everything, of their sharing with their family and camp and band, of the love and respect in which all the others of ^{n}dé held them. Creator told them that just as they had decided, so very many winters past, not to make anyone unhappy by forcing choice, neither would Creator leave anyone bereft. Right then, at that very moment, Creator took all three of them, together.

In the morning, the people of the camp were surprised to find all of them gone, all three of them, even though only the old man had been sick. As the bodies were prepared for burial, the shaman—the one who dreams and remembers, the one who visits The Real World of Creator and Power from This World of Shadows and Illusions— the shaman prepared by fasting and praying. There was a message the people needed that was not yet clear to him. He would learn what it was through his fast and prayers, through listening to the voice of Creator, whether it was in the wind, in his mind, through the words of another, or simply made manifest.

The message became clear the very next morning, as the shaman prepared to greet prayerfully the rising sun, the visible representation of Creator. There, in the eastern summer sky, just two handspans above the horizon was a new set of stars—three of them in a row. Instantly, the shaman realized they were those three who had lived together in such harmony and generosity all their lives. There, in the sky, Creator had placed them to serve always as a reminder of how ^{n}dé should behave. There they are today, The-Three-Who-Went-Together.

"That one like The-Three-Who-Went-Together" is enough to index the entire narrative. I had been told the narrative on several occasions through the years, and Lauren had grown up with it, as her children were doing now. One summer it became apparent to me that the stars making up the constellation Tainashka?da/The-Three-Who-Went-Together are, in English, Capella plus eta and iota Aurigae: three stars in the constellation Auriga, itself a part of Taurus.

There is much more than stars in the story, however. Referencing the story of The-Three-Who-Went-Together while I was eating was also a subtle lesson for Lauren's children, especially Nancy, who had not yet joined her siblings in front of the television.

Nancy is just learning about the Mescalero Apache beliefs and attitudes toward politeness, kindness, generosity, and reciprocity. She is just learning how one treats relatives and other members of the tribe. So it is good for her to be reminded of a model marriage in which not only was there respect for each other but also there was continuing generosity. She could see that her mother was treating me like an honored guest, as well as a sister, by providing food without being asked to do so.

It is considered impolite in the extreme for family members, in particular, to have to ask for anything. What one has simply is offered. Even the act of passing food is different than mainstream Americans expect. The hostess or host says, "I'm *offering* coffee and fry bread," for example. The guest, whether or not a family member, will not ask for honey or jam or eggs or anything else, because people always offer what they have to share. No one would dream of embarrassing another by asking for more than what had been offered.

Whenever I arrive or leave the reservation, I am plied with food. Food is prepared for me to take with me in the car, just in case I don't have enough money to eat properly on the road and also to be sure that we all realize we are family and are concerned for each other's welfare. Similarly, I also buy food (like sacks of flour, or pounds of coffee and lard and sugar, or big pieces of meat like whole hams) that I place in the refrigerator or in the other proper storage areas. And, when I leave, I usually leave $20 on top of the refrigerator. Families share with each other always.

The-Three-Who-Went-Together shared not just with family but also with the tribe as a whole. And that, too, is a positive quality that the young of today are taught. Apaches speak of their "Four Laws"—what might be considered right and proper conduct. Generosity is primary, for it is the most important of the four; it is the highest virtue. Following closely behind are bravery, honesty, and pride in oneself and one's people. With the use of the tag line referring to The-Three-Who-Went-Together, especially as one is eating, generosity is quickly indexed, as is pride for exhibiting proper conduct. Such lessons are not lost on the children, or on me, for that matter.

Reciprocity is the Anglo term for what Mescalero Apache people come to expect as natural and normal. A person does not keep a list of who owes what to whom or who gave what to whom. Rather, a person shares whatever is available to share, knowing that when there is nothing to share others in the community will provide what is needed. In this way, what goes around comes around. For example, if one of my family members has shoes with holes in them and if I have money, I buy replacement shoes. No one would ask me to do so, but people do pay attention to who needs what and, if possible, fills the need. It is highly unlikely that anyone will buy me a pair of shoes in return. But the next time I go to the reservation, it is quite likely that someone will have made me a dance shawl or a piece of jewelry. Reciprocity is often delayed, but it occurs nonetheless.

The trio in The-Three-Who-Went-Together are known to have been models for right and proper Apachean conduct. So a reference to them is also a reference to what makes a person a good person, in Apachean terms. The mythic present is at work vigorously in the lived present.

If Lauren had just used Betty's first name, I would have been confused about whom she was speaking. There is more than one older woman with that first name. But by saying, "that one like The-Three-Who-Went-Together," Lauren specifically referenced the particular Betty about whom she was speaking: the one in a polygynous marriage. The accessing of the mythic present in the lived present made which Betty she meant very clear. It is as though Betty, her co-wife, and their husband were also part of the original Three-Who-Went-Together. Time was collapsed into the present from the long ago and, simultaneously, the present was inexorably linked with the long ago: what was meaningful long ago is still meaningful now.

Of course, Mescalero Apaches, like all Native American people in the confines of the United States, live in accordance with United States law. They also live by the laws of the states in which they reside and the laws of the counties, too. But there is an older law, a body of traditional law, that claims their adherence as well. Today, polygamy of any kind is outlawed in the United States. But it is still practiced by some families from the Church of Latter-Day Saints, usually called Mormons, and by some Native American people. Such marriages are usually kept secret, except from the local community. Nowadays, at least at Mescalero, such marriages are no longer contracted. However, when I first went to Mescalero, in 1964, it was still possible to so marry—usually by having an Anglo ceremony with one wife and an Indian ceremony with the other.

All of this—the narrative, old traditional law, new laws, new customs—came to mind as Lauren mentioned "that one like The-Three-Who-Went-Together." The mythic present does a lot of work in today's life.

It was as though I had left only yesterday, listening to more than words and understanding that which is not said as well as that which is verbalized. We picked up the conversation about events that had happened since last I was on the reservation: who has had babies; who has died; which elderly people had to be hospitalized; who has started or stopped drinking; what the kids are doing in school; when to expect the rest of the family; and when we are moving to the mesa around the ceremonial arena.

This year the move had already started before I arrived. The family tipi had been erected, and some bed frames were already in. "I came back to get the mattresses and covers when it started raining here. It didn't look like rain up there, but I guess I'll wait until it stops. Don't want to get those mattresses wet," Lauren told me.

North, in this photograph, is at the upper right corner. Although the photograph is from about 1957, it looks like a ceremonial encampment that can be seen today. The line of tipis with tents beside them and domed arbors in front of them are the camp-out homes of the ceremonial girls. In front of them (to the north) is the long cooking arbor. Today's encampments also include pickup truck campers. (Photographer unknown; photograph reproduced by courtesy of the Museum of New Mexico, negative number 59303.)

"I smelled the rain on the way in, but I didn't see any clouds around the ceremonial mesa," I responded. "When you are ready, I'll go back up and help."

Lauren laughed and began teasing me, "Au. Like you helped with the chili and Harold's mother almost burned her mouth. Or like you helped with the tipi flap and all the smoke came inside. Maybe you better just go visit!"

Those two events, separated by years, had occurred when I was just acquiring skills that every proper woman has. If I still was learning, I would never have been teased, for that might cause me to cease trying and would embarrass me, an adult. No proper adult embarrasses another in public, for to do so causes the perpetrator to lose face. Even within the family, no adult even teases another unless embarrassment can be ruled out as a possible consequence of the teasing. What Lauren was telling me was that I was now accepted as a proper woman of the family who knew which relatives liked how much spice in their food and how to care properly for a home, whether or not it was a tipi. She was also giving me permission to leave her to work alone on the ceremonial mesa, rather than to help her set up our camp, and to go visit the many families with whom I like to keep in contact. Since the ceremonial is a time for homecoming, visiting among the camps is a common practice, especially for those of us who no longer, or never did, live on the Reservation.

"I'm supposed to take pictures for Hilda's and Sol's girl. Guess they are there already," I asked. Asking a direct question is impolite, except in the confines of family. Even within the family, it is better and more socially correct to ask without actually asking. By stating that I thought they might already be there, on the ceremonial mesa, I was actually asking which camp was theirs. Those girls who are having a ceremonial always have their camps set up first. So it followed that if Lauren was setting up her camp, then the camps of the feast girls, as they are also called, would already be set.

"They are the first, easternmost, camp. Our brother is singing for them." And, again, a vast amount of data is communicated by a small amount of talk. Lauren had told me that I would find Hilda and Sol, with their daughter, in a position that indicated that the head singer was singing for their girl, for the head singer's charge is always in the easternmost (considered to be the first) position. Not only was our brother,

Bernard, singing, but also he was still head singer, the one the other singers would follow in their four nights of song and four days and nights of ritual actions.

When the summer shower ceased, we packed up kids, mattresses and bedding, pots and ladles, the ice chest filled with Coors and Cokes, and my "anthropologist stuff"— cameras, film, notebooks, pens, tape recorder, and tapes. Jay, my son-nephew, took charge of the cameras, as he has since he was four years old. Children at Mescalero are trusted with responsibilities much earlier than are mainstream American children; and there was never any problem with expensive equipment in little hands. As a matter of fact, Jay had become a good photographer himself.

As we trundled up the ceremonial mesa in Lauren's pickup truck (cargo and kids in the back), we waved and tooted at friends and relatives, dodged the other trucks carrying evergreen and oak boughs to be used in people's camps, and stopped periodically to give or receive verbal messages. One such message was for me. Fernando's aunt said, "He said to tell you to go to his camp; they made tiswin/native corn beer."

Fernando is a longtime member of the Tribal Council who has been a friend almost from the first time I went to Mescalero. He is well educated and well read about his people. In addition, he researches and reproduces what they used to do. I assumed the venture into tiswin was one such research and practice project.

Tiswin was the only alcoholic beverage aboriginal Apaches had. And it is a late arrival into their culture. Most Mescalero people do not farm and did not do so in aboriginal times either. So their supplies of corn came in trade from the Puebloan people. Probably the recipe for making tiswin also came from them.

As soon as we had unloaded the pickup, I left Lauren to bring some order to the camp while I went to Fernando family's usual camp area, postponing for a little while going to Hilda's and Sol's camp to let them know I had arrived. I rationalized that they probably already knew, since little passes unnoticed in a small community, such as Mescalero, and since "moccasin telegraph" (kind of an each-one-tell-several communication system) is always working. Delores, my daughter-niece, walked at my side, chattering all the way. Delores, Lauren's middle child, is frequently my companion when I am at

Mescalero, and Fernando is one of her "uncles" in Indian terms and a distant cousin in Anglo terms.

"We're goin' visiting, huh, Auntie?" Delores queried. My response of, "Au," was enough to keep her talking. "Guess we'll be at Uncle 'Nando's." (It was easily assumed, as it lay directly in front of us.) "Guess that's where we're goin'. I'm gonna play with the boys."

But when we arrived, Delores suddenly became shy as she eyed the boys from the safety of my lap. As she accepted a proffered cookie, I sipped from the common dipper holding the tiswin. It is a bitter brew and, as I involuntarily made a face, people laughed and I was grateful for the cover of the wickiup in which we all sat so that I could hide my embarrassment.

Wickiups, or arbors, as they are more generally called at Mescalero, are common camp-out structures that do not vary with ethnicity. There are actually three ethnic divisions of Apaches who live on the contemporary Mescalero Apache Indian Reservation: Mescalero Apaches, Chiricahua Apaches, and Lipan Apaches. They are distinguished by certain lexical items (words or pronunciations of words), preferences for particular colors in body painting or in bead decoration on clothing, and by other minor variations in everyday lifestyle. However, they all share in common the dome-shaped wickiup/arbor.

When first I was going to the Reservation, many of the arbors were covered all over with tightly interwoven, freshly cut oak branches—the traditional way before the coming of the Anglos, Apaches aver. Those arbors formed a wonderful shade that allowed good air movement, providing a cool place to sit on hot afternoons. A fire in the center of the arbor could be used for cooking, or to guard against the chill of an evening or of a rain shower. If the rain was particularly strong, oftentimes water would drip in, but then people could go into a tent or tipi. Probably for this drippy reason, and also because it is easier and takes less time than carefully interweaving boughs all over the structure instead of just on the sides, people also used canvas tarps to cover the top of the structure. Of course, canvas was unavailable until Anglo contact times in the 1800s. Nowadays most people cover the tops of wickiups with plastic or heavy canvas tarps. The exception is the large cooking arbor of the girls' puberty ceremonial, the arbor where meals are cooked for the assembled guests and tourists. This large structure is still built in the traditional way, with a bent sapling frame and interwoven oak bough siding and roofing; this building style allows smoke from the cooking fires to escape no matter which way the wind is blowing.

The wickiup in which we sat was one of the old-fashioned variety, bereft of canvas tarp or plastic sheeting, for Fernando is a fine craftsman. That had already been evident in the tiswin that he had brewed. I could appreciate the excellent work exhibited in the tightly woven roof of the wickiup more easily than I could the bitter brew.

Sallie, Fernando's Mexican-American wife, and I caught each other up on what our children were doing and what had happened in our personal lives since last we had visited together the previous summer. She and Fernando had recently opened a restaurant with an attached arts and crafts store that kept them very busy. Making promises to stop by to eat at the restaurant before I left the Reservation, Delores and I sauntered back to Lauren's camp, stopping often to greet friends and meet new babies.

"You're here!" Bernard, Lauren's older brother, said to me as Delores and I walked into the family's tipi that Lauren had made shipshape. He rose to hug me and we chattered in a mixture of English and Apache, making arrangements for the rest of the day and those to follow.

He interrupted himself long enough to hiss at Delores as she started to walk around, in a counterclockwise manner, inside the tipi. "SSSSssssssss! Duuda!/No! Sunwise! Always walk sunwise inside kughą"/home. (Kughą carries the connotation of a proper home: that is, a tipi-home.) A chagrined Delores hung her head and immediately corrected herself, for she had heard this admonition many times before.

In a matrilineal society, such as the Mescalero one, only sisters and brothers, or those family members in the ascending generations, chastise or discipline children; providing discipline is considered to be inappropriate for a father, who has a strong emotional link with his children but who is in a different family. Fathers are sources of emotional and financial support and are not authoritarian toward their children. Nor is it appropriate for those outside the family to chastise or discipline children. Since sisters and brothers are always in the same family, it is the mother's brothers who are the disciplinarians, those with authority to help mold children into the proper form for Apachean cultural and social life.

Families are composed of matrilineages, lines that trace their relationship through mothers. In a matrilineage, women are the important links to determine one's family—those to whom one recognizes direct kinship through the blood (i.e., consanguinal kin)[2] and to whom one feels emotionally the closest.

The chart (Figure 2) is of my fictive family at Mescalero; therefore, I am indicated in it too.

So Bernard's correction of Delores's behavior was proper. He was the one in the family who first saw the infraction and so he was the one to correct it.[3]

Delores was so embarrassed at having to be reminded that I tried to gloss over the situation by announcing I was going to Hilda's and Sol's camp to let them know I was there and ready to photograph for them, thinking she'd accompany me as she had to Fernando's. But when Bernard said he'd go with me, Delores developed a sudden interest in the ice chest and a can of Coke, to be consumed, I supposed, to the Indian flute music of the tape she'd just selected from those lying near a portable player on the table. Bernard waited while I picked up my camera and checked to be sure it was loaded before putting it into my backpack along with the tapes, tape recorder, notebook, and pens.

Bernard's camp, managed by Lauren, is always south of the ceremonial arena where the girls' puberty events take place; our tipi is centered in the midst of the few others who camp in this area. The camps of the girls having their ceremonial are in front, to the north, of us. And in front of those camps, there is always the cooking arbor and the arena itself.

This year, Hilda's and Sol's camp lay at the eastern edge of the ceremonial mesa, since Bernard was the singer for their daughter, Stephanie. The head singer's charge is always in the easternmost camp (see Figure 3).

Bernard told me there were probably going to be lots of photographers who would likely only be there for the first morning—and maybe the last one. Stephanie is a direct descendant of Geronimo, so people expected (correctly, as it turned out) there would be great media interest in her puberty ceremonial.

Keeping track of male relatives may seem strange in a matrilineal society. But it is important to remember that all

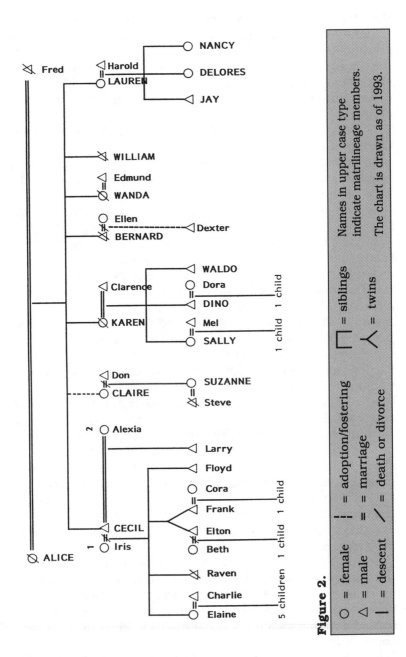

Figure 2.

O = female   ¦¦¦ = adoption/fostering   Names in upper case type indicate matrilineage members.

△ = male   = = marriage   ⊓ = siblings

| = descent   ╱ = death or divorce   ⋀ = twins

The chart is drawn as of 1993.

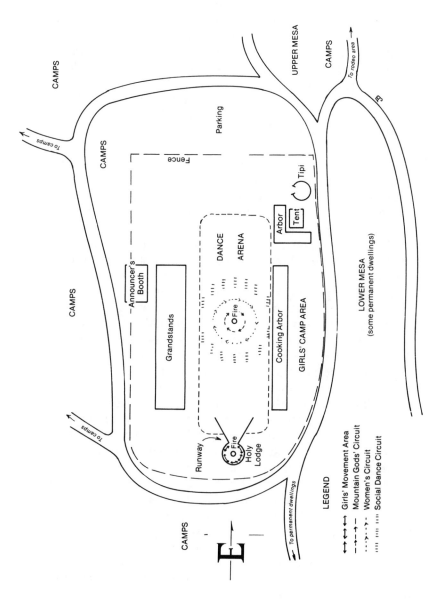

Figure 3. Typical plan of a ceremonial area. (See also Figure 4, page 60, for a diagram of the Holy Lodge/ceremonial tipi.)

those in one's matrilineage, whether or not they are female, are important. In this case, though, Stephanie's relationship with Geronimo is through her father; thus, in technical matrilineal terms, she is not related to Geronimo. But, in practical everyday terms, she is considered to be. People at Mescalero, and everywhere else throughout the world, often have discrepancies between their ideal behavior and their real behavior. Geronimo is famous; and for most people, being linked with the famous is desirable. Many people at Mescalero strategically invoke kin relationships, whether or not they fit the matrilineal mold.

Hilda and Sol had secured my camera permit—a plastic name tag with my name and Wendell Chino's signature; Anglos are not normally allowed to take photographs at a ceremonial. However, since my photographs were exclusively for the family and their use, rather than commercial or exploitive purposes, I had a permit. But even that permit usually does not allow photographing inside the ceremonial tipi.

As I pinned on my camera permit, Bernard told us what he wanted me to photograph and where he wanted me to stand at particular times during the ceremonial. Then Stephanie's parents made their requests for additional photos they wanted. Among those were some of their camp-out area of tipi, tent, arbor, and their cooking space in the long communal cooking arbor. I took the opportunity of relative inactivity in those places and immediately snapped those photos. Then I was reintroduced to Stephanie, whom I had not seen since she was a little girl, and photographed her. We parted from them with my promise that I would be there long before sunrise the next morning, the first day of the ceremonial.

Back in our own camp, I arranged my sleeping bag on one of the mattresses Lauren had brought. My place was directly opposite the tipi flap, the place for the owner of the home,[4] and where I had assumed Lauren would place her own bed. However, she and Harold had decided to sleep at the house, since Nancy (my youngest daughter-niece) seemed to be coming down with a cold. Because I was always very busy the morning of the first day, I asked her also to take Delores and Jay with her. Having recently been corrected by her uncle, Delores was eager to leave; but there was no budging Jay. He affixed himself to my side and stayed there, all the while promising to stay out of my way and be quiet (rather than bombarding me with questions, as usually he did), to be the best boy anyone had ever seen (instead of his normal self), to carry my cameras very carefully (instead of running with them), and only to take pictures when I said it was OK (instead of snapping his friends, aiming at the eagles that were too high to be caught with the lens, seeing if he could run and take pictures at the same time, or focusing on the tempting fast-food stands).

It was still warm, although it was late afternoon and the sun was beginning its descent behind the mountains. As we entered the tipi to rest, talk, and greet any visitors who might happen by, we noticed lightning striking in the desert to the west. The wind did not yet carry the smell of moisture, nor could we hear the distant thunder. But the storm was definitely moving our way.

As we stepped inside the shade of the tipi, Bernard went to the ice chest, handed Jay a Coke and opened a can of Coors/(joking called) Indian Kool-Aid for he and I to share; people in my Mescalero family tease me about wasting a good can of beer on me, since it usually goes flat before I finish it. Bernard picked up a piece of soft yucca stalk to fashion into some needed equipment and I settled down on my mattress. With my rolled-up sleeping bag as a back rest and camera bag as a desk, I turned on the tape recorder lying next to the Coors can between Bernard and me.

"Shilaa-n"/my sibling (literally, my hand, with the -n indicating that a person was intended), I said . . . and Bernard started to laugh. By addressing him as shilaa-n, when combined with the tone of voice, he knew I was going to ask him a favor that he would be duty bound, as my brother, to honor. He himself had taught me the power of invoking kin terms to get what one wanted and how to manipulate those terms to emphasize or call attention to a request. Since I had the tape recorder out and was reaching to turn it on as I addressed him, he knew that I wanted something pertaining to my work. I filled in the missing information with a request for a traditional story, "Maybe this is a good time to talk about things from the beginningtime." One only talks about things in context; the beginningtime stories are recounted throughout the four nights of the puberty ceremonial and so I thought it would be a time when I could fill in information or gather some new things he had not told me previously.

Perhaps it was because the sky was becoming cloudy and there was rain to the west or perhaps it was because it was a story I'd not heard before in quite the way he was to tell it this day or perhaps it was because Jay was present or perhaps it was in order to be sure to call the rain to the Reservation. Whatever the reason, he told Jay and me the following story.[5]

> These mountains was everything to us, as it is today. It was the center of our homeland; we traveled to the north; we traveled to the east, to the south. But this was the heart of our homeland. It had everything for us. We came here for our tipi poles; we came here to hunt our deer. We came here to refresh ourselves and for the medicine and things that we needed in our, in our lives. It was also here that we returned to seek visions from the high points of our mountains—that we would know and see in this world. This land is everything to us; this mountains is everything to us.
>
> In our sorrows, it puts happiness back in us. When the land itself is sad, we are sad with it and then it comes right back and it says, "Do not be sad, my children." For we are its children; we are its children. It was made for us and we roam around it, but we always return to it. As a child always returns to its parents, we return to our mother here, these mountains.
>
> The blueness and the richness that you, as you look into them, . . . means *something*. Not only is it food and a home, but it is also security. My people, they walk this land with a security that they have a home. They have something that is tangible. For everything else has been taken from us in this world. We became a conquered people. But this land is *our* land . . . rest assured that we will fight for it with everything that we have.
>
> When we walk on it, we look, we look around at the land and we see the vegetable food that it gives to us. When we look around, our relatives, the animals, they also see that vegetable food, for it is their food, too. This home is our home with our animal relatives. Our horses, our deer, our elk, our antelope, the turkey, ducks, goose: whatever this land has, we live in this country with it. Everything was given to us to live on; the bounties of this country is beyond belief . . .
>
> In the summer, in the summer when the rains come, the clouds would come from different directions—and they would bring forth rain. And they would pass through; and

the land was cheerful, happy, bright—and it was clean and fresh.

In the fall, when the little rains came, and they came to dry up the leaves for the winter, the land was saying something. It was saying, "Get ready! Get ready! For winter's comin'. Make your tipis warm. Make your parfleches heavy with food, for the winter will be hard." It said something, when the winds in the fall came out with the little rain. It said to get ready, to be prepared, to be on guard, for this was the time; it was a tricky time.

And then as it got into winter, the little snows would come. They were sharp and the wind would blow with them. And that means you'd have to stay, stay close to camp, stay close to home.

After that, the *big* snows came. The big snows came—not with a fierce wind but with a heavy, thick wind. And you were, if you were industrious, you were assured that you would weather the storm. But even the snow, with all its cold and its hardships that it brought, it was another thing. It said something to us—that this land was being refreshed by heavy snows and that it was putting moisture into the land.

And then spring would come. Spring, with all the plants would show their new faces to the world. And they were brave. And then you would understand what the snow, the big snows, were about: it was moisture that was being stored up. And this would be the beginning of plant life—which we all subsisted on.

As that went on into very late spring and early summer, the land would dry up; the land would dry up and it cracked. The land would crack and everything would be dusty. And even the people were dusty in their feelings, too. So they would pray; they would bring forth their dances and call out to the Four Directions of the Universe for help and say, "Help us! Our land is pitiful. We are pitiful. Help us." And the rains would come, the heavy summer rains, as they come now with the big, thick clouds coming over. [Now we could smell the rain.]

And Little Boy Lightning would herald them in; as they were coming in, he would be fierce and loud. And he would throw his arrows all over the land. And then a man should not . . . wander about. Horses knew better and would stand—not under trees—but somewhere where they would not be hurt by lightning.

And then Old Man Thunder, as you hear now [for, indeed, the storm was moving closer to us and we could now clearly hear the thunder and, even though inside, we were aware of ever closer and closer lightning strikes], he would come in. He would be like a voice saying, "Yes, I am God's generosity to you, my children." And he would give us the heavy rains and the land would burst forth with all the plant life. And both our animal relatives and we would be happy and our faces would brighten up . . .

When the two Spirit Warriors came out of the Sky, in the beginningtime, to give Lightning and Thunder to The People, the Thunder rode on a black horse and Lightning rode on a blue horse. They were the most handsome men that had ever been seen. And they had long, black, flowing hair and their heel fringes on their moccasins were long and flowing. Their gees [breechcloths] were long and flowing in back of them. The manes and the tails of their horses were fire and they were coming down to a people. They put forth their fingers, their hands on the left side [closest to the heart and therefore closest to Creator]. And the one on the black horse, from his fingers came thunder. And the Spirit Warrior on the blue horse, from his finger tips came lightning. That's how lighting and thunder came to a people.

And that's how Jay went to sleep, taking a nap before dinner, as the rain began to pelt the sides of the tipi; how the mythic present is part of the lived present; how rain, thunder, and lightning are presented; and how an arriving day was spent.

Notes

[1] When speaking Apache, Jay, Delores, and Nancy—the children of my fictive sister, Lauren—call me shimá/my mother or /my mama. When speaking English, they refer to me as "Auntie." These terms are in recognition of the two different kin systems in operation. In the Apache matrilineal system, one's siblings and first cousins through their mothers are all called by the equivalent terms for what in English is expressed by "sister" and "brother." In this matrilineal system, sisters (and, in English, female first cousins on one's mother's side) can and often do substitute for each other; so shimá recognizes my place in the family as a sister of the children's biological mother and therefore a woman who can appropriately also be termed mother. In the Anglo bilateral system, the children appropriately address me as a sister of their biological mother, that is, auntie. In order to incorporate both systems of kinship, in this book I refer to them as daughter-niece or son-nephew. While these are fictive relationships, they are nonetheless strongly affective ones.

[2] Literally, consanguineal means with the blood; the word is from two Latin roots: con/with and sang-/blood. While Apaches are fully aware of contemporary scientific biology, they consider their "blood relatives" to be those people to whom they are related through their mothers. Those relatives one receives through one's father are also recognized as being close, but they are not considered consanguines. Nevertheless, a person does not marry someone from a father's side despite their being considered to be from a different family.

[3] Bernard took his responsibilities quite seriously, vis-à-vis my daughter, Suzanne, after we were informally adopted into his family and became fictive kin. He often corrected her behavior, usually ending with, "You shame your whole family when you . . ." Many times he told her, "Our family is proud; don't . . . ," or "Remember, when people look at you, they look at our whole family," or "The women in our family always . . ."

Suzanne was almost fifteen years old before her sudden insight one day of, "Uncle Bernard loves me; that's why he's always telling me what to do." She said it with incredulity after reading an article—on the role of the mother's brother among the Hopi, also a matrilineal people—by my friend and colleague, Joann Keali'inohomoku. As it happened, Bernard was visiting us in Washington, D.C. at the time; when he returned that evening, Suzanne hugged him and told him she understood why he was "always yelling" at her (he never raised his voice to her, by the way); it was because he loved her. His comment, equally incredulous as her earlier one had been, was, "Of course. Why else would I bother? You are my sister's child. If I don't tell you, who will?"

[4] At Mescalero, homes and their contents belong to women.

[5] This story is abridged from the original tellings (July 29, 1975 and July 14, 1976). Bernard's first language was Mescalero Apache; his second was Chiricahua Apache; his third and fourth languages were Lipan Apache and Jicarilla Apache, learned at the same time; his fifth was Navajo; his sixth was English; his seventh, Spanish and the eighth, German. I have not corrected the English to the formal standard, preferring the flavor of so-called "Indian English." Although told originally to me in English, the narratives have a poetic structure. I have eliminated it here in favor of storyline only. See Farrer 1991 for examples of Bernard Second's poetic narratives.

Note also that Apaches know that calling Rain's ritual name in narrative results in calling the physical presence of rain to oneself.

3

On Forming Women
Ceremonial Day One

S is! Sis! Dii/here. Bizaaye lizhi ʔehųkaʔaʔitu''/a little coffee (literally, a small amount of black bittersweet water).

Bernard was gently but firmly insisting I awaken in the predawn darkness and make ready for the starting events on this first day of the girls' puberty ceremonial. As usual, his watchless and clockless time sense was impeccable, for we would have just enough time to do all that must be done before he moved into the ceremonial arena for the start of this July's ceremonial.

He had stirred the coals of last night's fire in the fire pit in the center of our tipi and had added wood, setting a bucket of water to heat on a makeshift grate and placing a blue and white enameled coffeepot by the pit's edge to keep it warm. It is well known in my fictive family that I am a grump without my morning coffee and even grumpier without a morning wash with warm, if not hot, water.

And, again, I was amazed at how I had learned not to hear that which did not concern me when in a tipi. I do not know when or how this occurred; I only remember being surprised

41

one day when I realized I no longer had to concentrate on not attending to things that were not my business and no longer even heard them. Usually, at home, I awaken at every little noise; but when I am sleeping in a tipi, someone can rekindle a fire, handle a grate, put a bucket on it, bring in coffee, and do who knows what all else without either my ears or nose being aware.

As I sat up in my sleeping bag, gratefully sipping the coffee, I noticed sleeping forms around the perimeter of our tipi. Seeing the sweep of my eyes and the focus on the huddled bundles, Bernard indicated they were the remnants of last night's party who had bedded down here. The one closest to the tipi flap was a Northern Plains Indian, a magnificent flute player whom I had not seen for several years and with whom I knew I would enjoy talking later. Closest to me were Wanda and Edmund, one of my fictive sisters and her husband; the others were a couple of men I did not know and did not meet.

Bernard began speaking in a normal tone of voice to awaken the others. It is inappropriate for men to be in a tipi while women wash, as my fictive sister and I would soon be doing. He announced, in a louder than necessary voice, that he must prepare for the morning's activities and that he needed his sisters' help in his preparations. That was a polite way of suggesting that the men leave but that the women remain, as we did.

Bernard took the coffeepot, cups, and sugar outside the tipi to a ramada/covered area (without walls) where the men could drink it at their leisure—after, of course, having physically left the tipi. Upon bathing and dressing, my sister and I left the tipi so that Bernard could get himself dressed before we affixed his ceremonial jewelry and he blessed us with tadidiin/cattail pollen.

I shivered in the shade of our extended family's ramada as I huddled close to the fire someone had thoughtfully lit while I checked camera batteries and loaded film and lenses into the pockets of my jacket: unexposed film in the left pocket, exposed film would go in the right; 35–105mm zoom lens on my favorite camera body and the telephoto lens on the other camera body. Fast film went into the camera with the zoom lens, for the photography would begin before daybreak; a slower film was loaded into the camera with the telephoto lens for use at certain points in the morning's activities after sunrise. I would write notes immediately after the morning's activities; by this time, I had seen a sufficient number of ceremonials managed by Bernard to know what was to come and so could be attentive to details of variations, as well as the girls' costumes and behavior: those things that I would want to be sure to put in my fieldnotes.

Bernard called Wanda and me into the tipi: one to fix his hair and insert his earrings and the other to polish the conchas (shell-shaped silver belt decorations) on his wide leather belt and to check his bandoleer (ritual, beaded sash worn over one shoulder and under the opposite arm) with its attached medicine pouch. Wanda was told to assist the women when it came time to raise the Four Grandfathers, as the main structure poles of the ceremonial tipi are called. I was again told to stand on the north side of the ceremonial arena and to take shots of particular activities: the singers quietly singing the morning songs; the pollen blessings to the Four Directions prior to that of the ground where the ceremonial tipi would rise; the measuring and laying out of the tipi circle; the pollen blessing of the poles; and on through the litany of scenes and events he wanted to be sure were captured on film.

The blue light of early morning seems particularly chill after a rain that persists intermittently throughout the night. Perhaps that is why there were only a few people in the grandstands surrounding the ceremonial arena. At this early hour, there are no tourists; they usually arrive after sunrise, and that was at least an hour away. Bernard was in the camp of the girl for whom he was singing, supervising the last-minute preparations. Wanda went into the cooking arbor for more coffee, and I went to sit in the north side grandstands to be in place for photographing as Bernard led the girl for whom he was singing into the ceremonial arena.

Gradually, the pace quickens as men who will assist in the raising of the ceremonial tipi come out of the cooking arbor and their own camps. Some begin carrying the twelve heavy, tall, evergreen poles that will soon become the ceremonial tipi. They lay them in a circle with an opening to the east, for it is crucial, at certain times in the ceremonial, that the full light of the newly risen sun shine directly into the center of the tipi.

Seemingly on cue, although no discernible one is given, the singers appear and begin their morning prayers and the pollen blessings of the ground, the place where the fire pit will be dug

The poles that will form the Holy Lodge/ceremonial tipi are arrayed on the ground as Bernard Second (with right arm outstretched) prays, facing east and offering cattail pollen. St. Joseph's Catholic Mission Church can be seen in the background. (Claire R. Farrer photo.)

in just a few minutes, and the poles of the ceremonial tipi. With the coming sunrise, the pace quickens. Accompanied by ululations of women, it is not long before the men begin erecting the Four Grandfathers: one pole for each of the cardinal directions.

When all Four Grandfathers are in place, they are leaned in toward one another and then are secured before the other eight poles are laid on and lashed in place. Then the covering is placed over the upper portion of the tipi, while simultaneously a wickiup weaving of oak boughs is interlaced on the bottom portion of the frame. Just before full sunrise, assuming the

The Four Grandfathers, one for each of the cardinal directions, just before they are leaned into each other and lashed together to form the tetrapod against which the other eight tipi poles will be laid for the ceremonial tipi. (Claire R. Farrer photo.)

Once the twelve tipi poles are in place, the canvas covering for the top of the tipi and the oak boughs to be interlaced on the bottom of the structure are quickly placed. (Claire R. Farrer photo.)

timing has been right, the entire structure is completed.

Meanwhile, the girls are being dressed and instructed in their camps. Each girl wears a special dress, made of soft skins. The dresses are embroidered with beads in exquisite designs of many colors; these patterns, in combination with the cut of the blouse and whether or not there is a toe guard (or turned-up piece on the front of the moccasins), indicate a girl's ethnicity: Mescalero and Lipan girls wear knee-high moccasins with plain-toed fronts, while Chiricahua girls' moccasins have a toe guard, a piece of skin that is turned up in the front of the foot and acts as a guard for the front of the foot. Skirts are heavily encrusted with cone-shaped jingles, made from food cans; not only do these make a pleasing sound as a girl moves, but also they add luster (and a considerable weight) to the costume. In addition, each girl has layers of necklaces—some gifts and some on loan from family and friends. There are a drinking tube (girls' lips do not touch water during ceremonial time) and a scratching stick (their hands do not come in contact with their bodies during this time) that are tied onto the costume with soft deerskin. A colorful scarf is tied so that it ripples down the back from its shoulder moorings and an eagle feather hangs in the hair, fastened near the crown of the head. Each item in the costume is reminiscent of White Painted Woman or Changing Woman, as she is sometimes called.

White Painted Woman is a culture heroine and the mother of the Warrior Twins, those beings who helped make the world fit for human habitation in the beginningtime. White Painted Woman, one narrative states, first appeared to ^{n}dé as a young girl walking in from the east. She reached adulthood, during which time she was associated with the south, the direction of soft winds and abundance, for she also taught many civilizing things to The People. As she aged, she was associated with the west—the direction taken by those who die. Finally, she was a very old woman indeed; at that time she was associated with the north. But, miraculously, after withering away, she appeared again, the very next day, as a young, nubile woman again approaching from the east.

In White Painted Woman's metaphoric journey among The People there is a lesson for today's women as well. New beginnings, among Apache people of the Mescalero Reservation, are associated with the east, just as the sun rises each day in the east. Particularly femininity, but also adulthood, are associated with the south, where the sun is said to be the warmest. The west is associated with sunset and the waning years of one's life, while the north is the area where the sun is the weakest and people are equated with being very old indeed. Just as White Painted Woman cycled through the lives of the ancestral Apache, today's girls cycle through their own lives: entering the Tribe as infants and being associated with the east; living out their productive and reproductive lives while being associated with the south; moving into "golden years" and grandparenthood with its westward associations; and finally, if lucky enough to live a complete life span, becoming white-headed and brittle-boned, they exist in north's home for a time, for the elderly are honored and highly respected in Apachean culture.

The girls' puberty ceremonial is celebrated after a girl has reached womanhood, for the people of the Mescalero Apache

Girls having their ceremonial are dressed as White Painted Woman, who is also called Changing Woman. Although this photograph is from 1960, today's ceremonial girls look the same in costuming. Note that the girl in ceremonial dress on the far left has moccasins with a turned-up toe, indicating her Chiricahua ancestry. (Photographer unknown; photograph taken July 4, 1960 and used here by courtesy of the Museum of New Mexico, negative number 111765.)

Reservation believe that a girl becomes a woman instantly upon initial menses. However, she is not necessarily a properly social woman, only a physiological one. The ceremony helps make her a proper social woman as well, although all acknowledge that a girl will become a woman with or without a ceremony.

During the time that White Painted Woman was on this earth, she was credited with showing The People much of what they know about health and healing. And during the time that a girl has her ceremonial, she is regarded as being a reincarnation of White Painted Woman. She, during the time of the ceremonial, will be sought out by those in need of special prayer or healing. Sometimes the girls merely bless such people; but other times there are reports of real cures happening. The girls are special indeed as they embark on the second stage of White Painted Woman's cycle and their own cycle within the social fabric of their Tribe. When the girls move into the ceremonial arena, they do so as living manifestations of White Painted Woman, with many of her powers on loan to them for a time.

Tules form a waiting carpet in front of the huge ceremonial tipi as each of the girls taking part in the ceremonial is led into the arena by her singer. Each girl is accompanied by her godmother, the woman who will guide her through the next several days and nights. The godmothers, sometimes assisted by a mother of a girl or another female relative, arrange blankets, quilts, and skins on top of the tules. The girls kneel, facing east, on the coverings on top of the tule carpet, their backs straight, their faces properly expressionless, as the pollen blessing exchanges begin: pollen cascades from fingertips first to the east, then the south, west, and north in succession before linking the circle thus defined with crossbars. The blessing replicates life's living circle: ⊕

The head singer is always the first to go through the line of girls. He kneels in front of each in turn, dips his thumb and forefinger into her pollen bag, and makes a blessing sequence with the pollen as he prays for her strength and success, not just for this day but for all the four days and nights of the rituals she will face, as well as for the rest of her life. She, in turn, blesses him. After the head singer, the other singers follow. Then it is the turn of the godmothers to pass through the line and exchange blessings with the girls. Finally, people in general pass in front of the girls to bless and be blessed. Those with special needs whisper them to the girls so that they may receive a special blessing and prayer. Infants who are too young to participate in the blessing exchanges have their hands guided by their caretakers; oftentimes, infants have their feet blessed, so that they will walk a proper path in this life, and have an infinitesimal amount of pollen placed in their mouths, so that they will speak properly in this life.

The pollen blessing sequence replicates not only life's living circle but also White Painted Woman's journey with its cardinal directions. It is all connected together by the crossings made from south to north (or from one ear to the other across the head) and from the center of the head to the forehead. Finally, there is a quick south-to-north movement across the bridge of the nose. All who participate in such a blessing sequence find themselves in the center of life's living circle.

If the girls seem to be getting tired or if there are just too many people in line, the head singer will motion everyone away so that the ritual may continue. Those who were not blessed in public will seek out the girls in their camp-out areas later in the morning so that they, too, may be blessed.

When the crowd has cleared, the singers step into the background while the godmothers come to the front. They lay their girls face down on the piles of blankets, quilts, and tules and, after smoothing their hair, begin to pray over them and massage them. This molding of the girls forms them into proper and beautiful women.

Next the girls rise, still facing east. The head singer brings out a deerskin that he lays on the ground. Carefully, he, or one of the other singers, begins a pollen painting of four crescent moons on the skin. Then the girl for whom the head singer sings moves onto the skin with her left foot while a song is sung; her right foot steps on the second of the crescents while another song is sung. Then, in turn, she makes two more steps to two more songs. Finally, she is pushed off the skin and begins her run to the east. The other girls follow her, each making four quick steps on the crescents and then running to the east. Each girl circles a basket that has been laid on the ground at the east entrance of the ceremonial arena.

Inside the basket are items that symbolically represent each of the four days of the creation. The basket itself represents industriousness.

At the conclusion of the first run, the girls return to their godmothers, who smooth their costumes if necessary, while another adult moves the basket a little closer into the ceremonial tipi. Again the girls run around the basket, while the godmothers set up a high-pitched ululation of keening, wordless, prayerful praise.

Altogether four runs are made around the basket. Each time the basket is moved closer to the tipi; this is a symbolic statement that although each girl is now a woman, her parents

Each ceremonial girl makes four runs around a basket on both the first and last days of the ceremonial. (Claire R. Farrer photo.)

wish to keep her close to home. The four runs that the girls make symbolize the four stages of life: infancy, childhood, adulthood, and old age.

At the conclusion of the fourth run, there is a frantic scramble to the front of the ceremonial tipi as burden baskets— filled with food, candy, money, and small items—are inverted over the girls. This action is a family's wish that the daughter being honored through the ceremonial will never want for anything. Children rush to pick up these goodies.

Almost simultaneously, pickup trucks move in front of the cooking arbor. From their beds, family members of the ceremonial girls begin to toss out more food and soft drinks, fruit and candy, and sometimes even small plastic household items. This time the scramble for the goodies includes adults as well as children.

The girls' singers and godmothers escort their charges back to their camp-out areas. Once there, the girls are ritually fed by the singers and godmothers, and then the head singer blesses the food that will be distributed to the waiting crowds; sometimes the girls, too, bless the food. The family of each ceremonial girl has prepared coffee and fry bread for breakfast. Some families also prepare traditional foods, such as mescal— the root of a giant agave and the carbohydrate source for which the Spanish named those we know today as the Mescaleros/ people of the mescal.

While the assembled crowd that has grown with the increased light of day eats breakfast, in the quiet of their camp-out homes the girls bless those who were not blessed publicly and the singers retire to their own camp-out areas to rest, to visit with newly arriving friends and family, and to prepare other ritual items that will be needed throughout the remainder of the ceremonial. Our family meets in our own tipi and those of cousins who always camp next to us.

Usually our family compound consists of three tipis and a shady ramada; in some years there is also a tent. Somewhere between twelve and twenty of us usually occupy the tipis and socialize in them and in the ramada, while the tent, when present, is just for sleeping. It is a time of teasing, learning, eating, relaxing, and just plain enjoying one another all together. This year is Delores's turn to be instructed, since she is now considered old enough to begin to understand parts of the ceremonial.

"Those girls run four times around that basket," her Uncle Bernard begins as she comes into the tipi munching a piece of fry bread. He glanced at her as she moved over to sit on his lap, leaning her head against his chest as he continued:

> They do that because of ʔIsdzanatłʔeesh/White Painted Woman. My grandparents told me these stories; if you call me a liar, you call them a liar.[1]

They say ʔIsdzanatłʔeesh first came to us from the East. Oh! She was beautiful, a beautiful young woman. She lived with us. She showed us many things. She grew to full adulthood and lived down there. [He gestured with his lips to the south.] She had children there. Then she became old, very old. Soon she would begin her westward journey. But first she became even older with thinned skin and white, white hair, hair like the snow in the north country where our people used to live.

[Delores turned her head and glanced at me and my gray-white hair, a gesture not lost on her uncle.]

She was much older than your auntie, much older. She walked on three; she walked with gish/cane. Then one day, she died. The People were so sad; we were sad, for we loved her dearly. But, we were surprised, too. All of us were surprised, for the next morning, the next sunrise, she appeared to us in the east again, a young woman again.

That's who those girls are: ʔIsdzanatłʔeesh. They go around that basket four times, just like she lived four stages in her life on this earth. Just like all of us live four stages: first we are babies, infants, like Nancy; then we are children, like you [and he patted Delores's shoulder]; then we are adults, like me and auntie; and, if we are lucky and live good lives, we become the elderlies, like Grandma Apache. That is a good life.

That's what my grandparents told me.[2]

Delores whispered something to Bernard I could not hear. "Of course!" he responded, "Of course you will be ʔIsdzanatłʔeesh. But I won't sing for you. Oh, no! I want to dance at your feast!" And Delores skipped out of the tipi giggling at the imagined sight of her very proper uncle dancing.

I settle in to write rough field notes, only to be interrupted by the screeching of someone's boombox. Such electronic gadgets on the ceremonial grounds always anger Bernard. He says he prefers only traditional things on the ceremonial grounds. I never mentioned that the cars and pickup trucks, to say nothing of the pots and pans used in our family, are hardly traditional. There are some things one does not mention.

Lauren and Harold came in with Jay and Nancy, Jay, as usual, begging for more money to spend on trash and junk food. This time, though, he insisted there was good jewelry at a stand set up by a Navajo family. That piqued both my interest and Bernard's, so we went to investigate, of course with Jay in tow.

Jay was right. There was excellent jewelry being offered by a Navajo family. Sometimes the concession stands are full of junk and other times, as on this day, there are real treasures offered. We bargained for a ring that Bernard particularly liked; when I bought it for him, he used it as a slide for his neckerchief.[3] Jay settled for a big cotton candy, finding no jewelry that suited him and not finding anyone selling the miniature bows and arrows that most of the little boys liked to carry around with them. I suspect, however, he was only exercising a strategy to get both candy and toys for, later in the afternoon, during the powwow dancing, he dragged me to the opposite end of the concession stands where there was a vendor with the miniature bows and arrows. Jay is clever when it comes to getting his relatives to buy him what he wants.

The ceremonial, with its myriad ritual activities, is done primarily at night, except for the first and last days, when there is also early morning activity. Afternoons are filled with a variety of activities. Recently, a Fourth of July parade has been added to the festivities. For many years there have been afternoon powwow dancing and a rodeo going on at overlapping times. The rodeo is part of the Indian cowboy circuit, so the riders and ropers can garner points for accumulation toward the year's Best All-Around Indian Cowboy. The powwow dancing always features at least two guest drum groups and substantial prizes in the various dance categories. Afternoons are filled with activities in addition to the usual ones of eating and visiting.

Women often fill their ceremonial days helping to prepare food. A girl's matrilineal family, sometimes extended matrilaterally as well, is expected to help with the cooking and serving. Affinal kin help, too, as do female friends, for there are massive amounts of food cooked each day. Just about everyone female spends some time chopping, mixing, washing, peeling, cooking, cleaning, serving, and visiting in one camp-out area or another.

Each camp-out area for each ceremonial girl resembles a restaurant's kitchen and storage facility. Twenty-five-pound sacks of flour are stacked almost as high as a person. Three-pound coffee cans and ten-pound lard cans form tables on which are set ten- and twenty-pound sacks of potatoes and huge sacks of sugar. Eggs by the crate and large slabs of meat are on hand, the meat usually slaughtered from the tribal herd of Herefords. There are chili ristras (two- and three-foot long strings of dried chili), as well as pounds and pounds of fresh, green chilis. Dozens of burlap sacks filled with dried pinto beans stand ready, along with boxes of paper and plastic plates and plastic cutlery on which are placed disposable cups by the hundreds. Cartons of fruit cocktail, scores of watermelons, lugs of peaches, and restaurant packs of Kool-Aid in various flavors are all in place. Many families also provide traditional wild foods of mescal root, mesquite beans, Indian bananas, and venison. All this food, and more, is necessary, since everyone who attends a ceremonial is fed three meals each day at no charge. It is an enormous expenditure for a family, even when the tribe as a corporate entity contributes toward the total.

There is an equal, if not greater, expenditure of human effort to turn the raw materials into delicious cooked meals. Breakfast always consists of coffee and fry bread. Fry bread—made from flour, salt, and water—must be mixed and kneaded, then allowed to rest and rise before being formed into rounds that are popped into boiling lard to be cooked. On the first and last days of the ceremonial most families also offer traditional foods for breakfast as well.

Lunch and dinner preparations begin as soon as the previous meal has ended. Vast chili stews of meat, chili, potatoes, and water cook in new twenty-gallon aluminum trash cans that are set next to or on grates over open fires. Other equally large cans are filled with beans and water, usually with pieces of salt pork added for flavor. Sometimes there are vegetable stews as well, with or without chili added.

Meanwhile, in the ramadas behind the large cooking arbor, family members and friends boil eggs and potatoes and chop celery, pickles, and onions for potato salads. Others wash head after head of lettuce and dozens of tomatoes for a green salad while their friends and family chop peppers and carrots to add. Still others concentrate on mixing the gallons of Kool-Aid while someone is detailed to go to town to buy more sheet cakes and cut them into serving pieces. Sometimes children are given the jobs of washing fresh fruit or cutting up melons or just opening can after can of fruit.

Preparing and serving the meals is a tremendous task that

requires lots of friends and relatives. Those Mescalero people who help are actually engaging in reciprocity; one pays back the families who helped one's own family members with their feasts and one builds credit, as it were, for the time when one's own daughters or nieces will require help for their feasts. Other Indian women from other reservations also help and, in return, receive help at their homes during their own feast times. Oftentimes Anglo women help, too; some work for the prestige it offers them and to learn how to make the various dishes that are so different from Anglo cuisine. Others help in families with whom they have friendship ties. Each woman gains while each one becomes exhausted and hot over boiling lard or testy over dishpan hands and arms and elbows.

Sometimes I help cook, and sometimes I just photograph those who are doing the work. Since photography is not considered proper work at Mescalero, it seems I also end up baby sitting when I am photographing rather than cooking, and I have learned that child care is an activity that does not always go well with photography. But I keep getting the job, though sometimes maybe not the picture.

Whenever possible, I try to take a nap in the afternoon, because Bernard always insists that I stay up, standing behind him, as he sings in the ceremonial tipi. Nights are busy even when the time in the ceremonial tipi is brief. The songs take a few hours to sing, even on the shortest of the singing nights. The Mountain Gods dance, usually between about 8:00 P.M. and midnight; and I like to see them, too, as do Apaches themselves and tourists. I also like to dance with the women who follow one group of Mountain God dancers and their drummer and chanters as they sing and dance their last song around midnight or so. Then, when we could, Bernard and I would usually stay up until two or three in the morning, discussing what I've seen or heard. Or he would take me outside to teach me more about the night sky. A nap becomes almost a necessity. However, getting one in the tipi is sometimes impossible, since it is always a center of activity. So somewhere around mid-afternoon, I try to sneak away back to Lauren's and Harold's house for a shower and a nap— sometimes I'm successful and sometimes not.

Regardless of whether or not a nap is actually achieved, I join the women of the family around 4:30 in the afternoon, in helping in one girl's camp or another—often by serving food.

The dinner lines are especially long, since many people come in the late afternoon to watch the end of the powwow dancing and to be in plenty of time for the dancing of the Mountain Gods.

The Mountain Gods are, most people say, a relatively recent but extremely important addition to the girls' puberty ceremonial. They dance to heal and to bless. In the not so distant past, there were many groups of dancers; now they are reduced in number. But they are spectacular nonetheless.

A Mountain God dancer is covered from the soles of his feet to more than two feet about his head, save the palms of his hands. Exposed skin is painted with symbolic designs that vary with the dictates of the owners of the sets of dancers. Some of the designs were being used generations ago and some are new, the result of a new vision or dream. High moccasins adorn feet; again, a turned-up toe indicates a Chiricahua man while a plain-toed moccasin indicates a Mescalero or Lipan man, for all the Mountain God dancers are men or older adolescent boys. A-line deerskin kilts are fastened around waists with wide belts, to which bells are attached. Streamers, each bearing four eagle feathers, are tied to upper arms. Heads are completely covered with tightly fitting cloth or skin, having small holes for eyes and mouth. Above the heads are elaborate headdresses that seem to take on a life of their own as the dancers bob and weave in stylized, stomping steps. They, and the vocal and drum music to which they dance, are mesmerizing.

Upon first entering the ceremonial arena, the Mountain God dancers bless the central fire around which they dance. On the first night of the ceremonial, they next bless the ceremonial tipi. They then begin their captivating dancing.

While they are dancing, and after full nightfall, the girls are led into the ceremonial tipi by the singers. Most people do not actually see this small parade, since their attention is riveted to the Mountain God dancers. But once inside the tipi, when the fire is lit in the firepit and the singing to deer hoof rattle accompaniment begins, people notice that the girls are present, and they begin to crowd around the entryway to the ceremonial tipi. They press against the sides, peering in through the interwoven boughs. Excitement is high and spreads quickly through the crowd.

On this, the first night, the songs refer to the first of the four

While in the ceremonial arena, Mountain God dancers are always in motion. These dancers have their backs to the camera; nonetheless, their headdresses, body painting, sashes, and arm streamers can be clearly seen. (Claire R. Farrer photo.)

days of Creation. While the singers sing of the beginningtime, the girls dance on cowhide mats. The jingles on their costumes, combined with the noise of their shuffling feet, produce a counterpoint to the men's voices. Godmothers sit close by their charges, interpreting the words of the songs, for they are sung in an archaic form of Apache that is quite different from the spoken language. Godmothers also massage the girls' legs and feet while encouraging them to dance for all of the songs sung, although such dancing is both strenuous and very taxing for the girls. Their physical sacrifice, however, is an important part of the ceremonial.

Usually, after the singing and dancing in the ceremonial tipi on the first night, the girls join the phalanx of women who dance in support of the Mountain Gods. The women's circle is several feet removed from the pathway of the Mountain Gods. Women dance in matrilineal groups, always with their upper bodies covered by a shawl that drapes over their shoulders and is held together in front by the women's hands hidden in the folds of fabric. The steps they do requires movement only from the knees down; such movement produces an undulation of the fringing on the women's shawls that is almost hypnotizing to watch. But the deceptively simple dance step is nearly as tiring as that which the girls do in the ceremonial tipi. The women and girls dancing in support of the Mountain Gods can stop whenever they tire, while the ceremonial girls are expected to dance at all times when there is music inside the ceremonial tipi. When dancing with the Mountain Gods, however, the ceremonial girls usually make only a few circuits of the fire before retiring, while the other women and girls dance as long as they wish.

By 11:30 or midnight, the girls are very tired. They have been up since long before dawn, have been involved in intensive rituals throughout the morning and night, and are more than ready to retire. As am I. When finally I snuggle down in my sleeping bag, valiantly trying to finish up a few notes by firelight, I go to sleep watching the stars spin through the open smokehole of the tipi and finding that once again my heartbeat has synchronized itself to the drumming of the Mountain Gods' music.

It is a lovely way to be lulled to sleep.

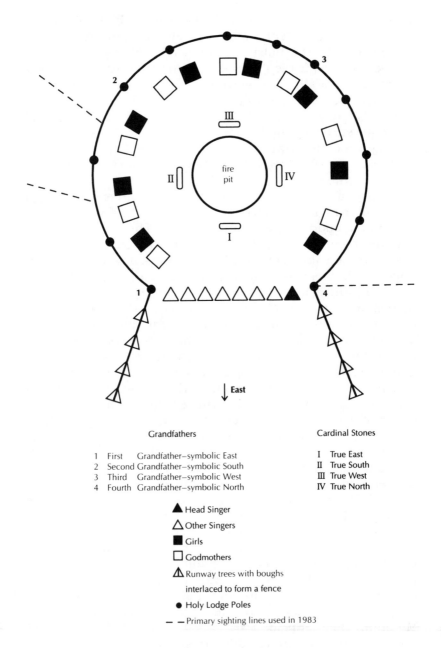

Figure 4. Diagram of the Holy Lodge/ceremonial tipi.

Notes

[1] Verbal recourse to the grandparents as well as the mentioning of lying are narrative formulas that inform an Apachean audience that the narrator is telling the truth and that the narrative to be told is to be accepted as a truthful, and often traditional, story.

[2] Ending a narrative with recourse to grandparents lends veracity to what has come before; it, too, is a narrative formula.

[3] The bargaining was between Bernard and a Navajo man and was held in a mixture of Navajo and Apache. When a price had been agreed upon, I took out the money. Then the Navajo man told me, in English, that the price was almost double what he and Bernard had just agreed upon. I said, "Duuda!/no!" while Bernard said, in Navajo, that the price just quoted was not the one agreed upon. The Navajo man responded, in Navajo, that the price he and Bernard had agreed upon was the price for Indians—Anglos paid more. Bernard, speaking Navajo, objected and said, "She is my sister." The Navajo demurred and denied the claim. So Bernard said to me, in Apache, "Tell him what we have been talking about." I gave an English précis of their conversation, including the disagreement over price. The Navajo man stared at me incredulously and stated that I just did not look Indian and Bernard replied, in English, "Different fathers." That was certainly true; what Bernard neglected to say was that we also had different mothers and that I was but a fictive family member.

I have often wished I could find that Navajo man again and tell him he had indeed been correct, but, then, saving close to $20 kept me from looking too hard.

4

"Koʔio!"/Go Around!
Ceremonial Day Two

Since there are no morning ritual activities for the girls on either this day or the next, they are considered more restful than the first or last days. It is usually a time of visiting. Unfortunately, it is also a time of drinking.

Alcoholism is an increasing problem on most Indian reservations today, and the Mescalero Apache Indian Reservation is no exception. When I was first at Mescalero in the early 1960s, it was rare to see an inebriated person on the ceremonial grounds. By the 1970s, drunken men were all too common, even at ceremonial time. By the 1980s, women, too, were publicly drunk. And now it seems the epidemic is fast consuming even the young.

Some authorities attribute the prevalence of alcoholism to a genetic biochemical anomaly among Native North Americans that makes it difficult for them to break down alcohol in their systems. Scholars of alcoholism in other disciplines also study the genetic aspects of the disease in all alcoholics and their families. Others attribute the alarming rise in alcoholism to a disparity between economic opportunities on most reservations and in mainstream America. Still others, and these are

63

becoming anachronistic, attribute it to a weakness of character. (This latter, highly judgmental, approach should probably also be studied in itself.) And there are some who attribute the problem to a lack of committed Christianity among reservation residents. It is important to keep in mind that there is also a more open attitude toward discussion of alcoholism at Mescalero than I have experienced in non-Indian communities in this country; so it is difficult to know whether alcoholism is actually more prevalent or simply more openly admitted to and discussed. I suspect this openness and discussion occur because Mescalero attitudes toward adult behavior differ from mainstream attitudes: at Mescalero an adult is responsible for her/his own behavior; the responsibility does not lie with one's background (deprived or privileged), family, spouse, friends, or any other outside influence. Therefore, there is no shame in discussing alcoholism; it is considered a disease that some have and others do not. Whatever the reasons—and I do believe one day it will be generally understood that the etiology of alcoholism has plural rather than singular causation—there is certainly more alcoholism present at Mescalero today then when first I went there to live in 1974.

That is not to say alcoholism was absent in the early 1970s; it was there and already extracting a toll. The first fetal alcohol syndrome child I ever saw was an infant at Mescalero in 1975. There was, and is, an alcohol rehabilitation center on the Reservation.

For many years the Tribal Council and groups of concerned citizens of the Mescalero Apache Indian Reservation have sought ways of decreasing the accidents and deaths directly attributable to alcohol. There are alcohol educational programs in place. There are carefully planned recreational activities designed to fill time that might otherwise be spent in drinking. After much discussion and agonizing over whether or not it was the right decision, the Tribe secured a liquor license and opened an Indians-only bar and lounge on the Reservation in a vain attempt to limit car accident-related injuries and deaths by having a local source of alcohol rather than having only distant ones in the non-Indian communities several miles away on both the west and east sides of the Reservation.

The probability of encountering drunks on the roads or on the ceremonial mesa is highest on the second and third days of the ceremonial. That always sets up ambivalence in me: on the one hand, I want to visit but, on the other, I dislike intensely dealing in any way with drunks. Deciding to risk it and stay and visit rather than find an excuse to be elsewhere, I went to Hilda's and Sol's camp to help with food preparation to see whether the family wanted a picture of themselves with Stephanie. Stephanie was resting, but Hilda indicated she really wanted a picture of herself and her daughter, as well as one of the three of them. Sol was busy at one of the cow camps, where he was helping slaughter beef for the remaining meals to be cooked, but Hilda thought he would be back by mid-afternoon. So I settled in to wait and make myself useful by helping to make fry bread.

"I guess jeans are just the worst, when you're cookin' fry bread," one of the older ladies said to me. She was right; I had forgotten how the denim seems to attract and hold heat. All the experienced ladies cook fry bread in dresses or lightweight cotton slacks for good reason. I felt as though the rivets in my Levis were making permanent scars on my body, and I couldn't find a stick long enough to remove me far from the fire and still allow me to turn the fry bread cooking in boiling lard. By common and unspoken agreement, I do not pat out the fry bread, for I have never learned the technique of making the dough come out in lovely rounds, as it should properly be. Mine always resembles a bell more than a circle. And, since the bread had been mixed long before I arrived and had been rising, there was little else to do but place the bread over a long stick, transfer it to the boiling lard, watch until it bubbled and became fluffy, and then turn the bread over to finish frying. And that meant roasting me while frying bread.

Louisa, an old and dear friend, came to my rescue after twenty minutes or so by patting the bench beside her where she was quickly turning out one perfect round of fry bread after another. "Come and sit. There are things we have to say to each other," she noted. Gratefully, I handed my turning stick to a properly attired lady and went to join Louisa on the bench far from the fry bread fire.

"Maybe you'd like some coffee while you do that," I volunteered.

"Au. That would be good," she agreed.

I went over to where a stew was simmering for the evening meal and a coffeepot sat invitingly on a grate. Sugar and styrofoam cups had been conveniently placed on a small table nearby. Taking two cups, and liberally lacing them with sugar, for camp coffee—cooked by putting grounds and water in a pot and boiling them together—can become as strong as espresso, I looked around for something to put on the hot handle to protect my hand from burning. A cloth for just this purpose is usually available, and I saw one about head height only a few steps away. As I took it and turned to step back to the coffeepot, a very obnoxious drunk man stood challengingly between me and the coffeepot. Such confrontations always fluster me: I don't want to be rude, since I am, after all, only a guest, but I also don't want to interact with drunks. Summoning my best matriarchal manner and eschewing Anglo manners while exercising my Apache ones, I said, "Go away, Old Man!" as I moved around him.

Again, Louisa came to my rescue, chastising him in Apache. He backed off long enough for me to fill the two cups and leave the cooking arbor, although we could hear him muttering behind us for a while in Apache, saying how Anglos never knew when to stay home. In a voice louder than was truly necessary, Louisa allowed as how neither did drunks and that some Anglos were invited guests, unlike drunks. Part of me silently thanked Louisa—and at least a little bit cheered her on. But I have a problem with this kind of incident, which somehow deeply embarrasses me. So, perhaps too eagerly, I changed the subject to a discussion of dancing and how lovely the women had looked the night before as they danced in support of the Mountain Gods. Louisa said she'd seen me last night, but that I was busy with him, meaning Bernard, but that tonight, since it would be a short night in the ceremonial tipi, I should come and dance with her and her sisters and their girls. I said that I would.

Louisa is an old and constant friend. She is the Mescalero woman who made me my first dance shawl in 1974; she and her sisters had been among those who had helped me to learn to dance Apache women's style.

Dance talk gave me an opportunity to relate how Anglo cleaners in California, where I live, do not know how to deal with Apache shawls. Shawls are usually made of double knit these days and, while the background fabric is washable, much of the decoration—it may be of felt, or beaded, or of satin—is not. In addition, shawls have long fringes of a nonwashable, synthetic fabric. I related how, in preparation for this ceremonial, I had taken my shawl to be cleaned only to have the cleaner balk, fearing that the fringes would be tangled and the shawl ruined. My assurances that such had not happened in the past were in vain. So, in order to have the cleaners accept the shawl, I had to stand there and braid well over eight feet of fringing that bordered my shawl. When I had finished the braids, the shawl looked as though it had been in the hands of one who prepares elaborate African-American hairstyles. Louisa later shared the story with her sisters, who teased me that night about spending more time on my shawl's "hair" than I did on my own. It is always a joy to see and laugh with Louisa and her sisters.

As we enjoyed our visit, the humidity had been rising for almost an hour, and the sky was beginning to threaten rain again. Excusing myself from Louisa with the real excuse that I had to take some pictures before the rain came, I went to Hilda to say that if we wanted to photograph today, we might want to do so before the rain began, so that Stephanie would not be in mud. As we discussed the best backdrop, finally settling on the side of the tipi, Sol arrived with a load of meat. Hilda told him I was there to take their family picture. While he went to clean up his hands and change his shirt, I photographed Hilda and Stephanie together; then Hilda, Stephanie, and her godmother. Finally, all was ready and, moments before the sky became really dark, I took the family portrait.

Bending low over the camera, for it was such a beautiful day when I'd left our tipi that I'd not taken a jacket or sweater with me, I hurried back to the security of our warm, dry, camp-out home. Rain is a marvelous blessing in the American Southwest, but it is certainly a mixed one during the girls' puberty ceremonial. If there is too much rain, or rain at the wrong time or place, the ceremonial will have to go on hold, disrupting people's schedules and causing anxiety. While rain is always needed—even in the mountains—in the arid Southwest, it is not wanted in large quantities on the ceremonial mesa during ceremonial time. It is considered to be truly wonderful if it rains all around and not on the mesa itself. But that was not to be this day, as the first huge, separate, well-spaced drops splashed on me even before I could go the few hundred yards from Hilda's and Sol's camp to our own.

As I hurried back toward our tipi, I could see people tying down the tipi flaps close to the tops of the poles, leaving only a small opening for smoke to escape; securing tipi door flaps against the wind; moving chairs into rustling arbors; pulling plastic taut over arbors and ramadas; checking tent pegs; examining cars and pickup trucks for stray children before closing them tight against the coming storm. And from past experience I knew they were also stirring tipi fires to renewed life; finding boots (or wishing they'd brought some from home); finding sweaters and jackets; and settling in for the now thunder-promised rain.

Maybe Bernard would be telling more stories in our tipi, since the thunder was crashing around the mesa with a sudden fury now. One only speaks of things like thunder when they are present; to speak of them in other times may well call them to you. Few consider themselves powerful enough to command nature and stand the consequences.

Since the sky was turning very dark, a heavy masculine rain could be expected. In general, dark colors are thought to be stronger and masculine, and light colors are usually more closely associated with femininity. Not that Apache women are weak—far from it. As I thought about the color business and color associations with directions, I had to remind myself that, like so many things at Mescalero, the attributes and associations of color might well be idiosyncratic. My understanding of them comes from Bernard, a powerful and respected singer among his people. But Bernard's vision might well be his own. I know he learned it from his grandfathers, but how much of it was shared in general among The People, or even the other singers, I did not then know. No singer will correct another's vision; a multiplicity of understandings is necessary, in the minds of most Mescalero people. Since the other singers knew of the relationship between Bernard and me, no one of them would contradict his versions to me. At the most they would say that they learned things a little differently, but not be specific. And certainly no people who are not religious specialists, as are the singers, would presume to correct a singer; a person might say that their own grandfathers said X rather than Y, but that would be the extent of it. Making a mental note to check on this sometime, I scurried on to our tipi.[1]

Jay was just closing the tipi flap against the rain as I came

barreling in. "Auntie sure is moving fast today," he teased.
"Fast enough to run over little boys who stand in the way,"
I responded.

He grinned and came to sit next to me as I checked the
camera for water and put it away while getting out my
notebook. A moment or two later, Nancy blustered in, looking
somewhat bedraggled and wet, and then shyly she retreated
a step or two backward, for there were many strangers inside
the tipi, people who had been visiting with and talking to her
Uncle Bernard while the others in the family were bustling
about on their own business. Not seeing her parents, and
apparently deciding I was too far away to be a safe haven, she
tried to make herself inconspicuous by backing to the edge of
the tipi, her thumb going toward her mouth and her left hand
reaching for the tipi wall.

"Duuda!" Bernard hissed at her. He barely looked up as he
continued to carve the sticks that would be used to count songs
sung on the last night of the ceremonial. Most of the people
probably had not seen her tiny hand move, but Nancy
understood and pulled her hand back, looking as though she
might cry, probably from embarrassment at being corrected
in front of strangers and from the disorientation she obviously
felt at finding so many of them in her own camp-out place.
Seeing her quavering, Bernard continued, "Dii", he said, as
he patted a spot next to him and reached for a towel to dry
her face and hair and a Coke to give her to lessen the impact
of his earlier sharp rebuke. As Nancy settled in and leaned
against her uncle's thigh, still eying the strangers, he began
talking. It seemed at first that he was talking to no one in
particular, but actually he was addressing her.

> In the old days, my grandparents told me, in the old days,
> children could touch the sides of tipis, if they wanted to.
> Then we made them of strong hides, buffalo hides. We put
> grasses behind those hides, in between the outside hides
> and the inside ones. Then, on the inside, we put soft
> deerhides. We had good insulation then and children could
> touch them. Now we just have canvas. We don't have any
> hides anymore. Just one layer of canvas between us and
> the wind, between us and the rain. No tough hides; no soft
> hides. Just canvas. When children touch canvas, it makes
> a place where the water can drip in. It was better in the
> old days, in the days my grandparents told me about. In

the days before the whiteman. In those days, children could touch the sides of tipis and the rain stayed out. It is not like that anymore.

Although she had been chastised, Nancy was now all smiles, for her uncle had tenderly diffused the embarrassment for her. It was not her fault tipis are made of canvas; it was not her fault children could not touch them. It was not her fault it was not the old days.

Probably remembering her own difficulties of the day before, Delores also chimed in, lecturing her younger sister, "And when you are in your camp-out home, when you are in kughą, ko?io/go around, ko?io. We always walk sunwise in here. We don't touch walls and we walk sunwise," she said as she gestured the proper, clockwise direction, "Go around."

Going around in a sunwise direction is ubiquitous. It can be seen repeatedly in the actions in the girls' puberty ceremony as the girls circle the basket in a clockwise manner, in the way they enter and progress inside the ceremonial tipi, in the form of the circle with embedded cross of the pollen blessings, in the dance patterns traced by the Mountain God dancers and the women dancing in support of them, even in the way in which salt is applied to food.

Not only are sunwise motions appropriate in the ceremonial, but also they are proper in daily life. Bernard taught me that sunwise directionality, and circularity itself, are from the Apachean religious philosophy; that, in turn, is based on astute observations of the natural universe and the sky in particular. Sky watchers quickly realize that stars and planets seemingly inscribe vast circles on the dome of the sky.

From the observations, both the philosophy (principles and concepts of knowledge) and epistemology (origin of human knowledge) of the people were devised. These are encoded in what I term a "base metaphor." The base metaphor, for the Mescalero Apache, includes circularity and sunwise directionality, balance and harmony, patterned sound and silence, as well as the number 4. All this is encapsulated in a design that is elegantly simple yet incorporates, mnemonically, all that is important in terms of Mescalero Apache values and propriety—a quartered circle: $\oplus$, the same form reproduced each time a pollen blessing sequence is done.

Some of the manifestations of roundness are subtle, as in

salting of food or as in the round corrals that can be seen on the Reservation. There is also the going-aroundness of reciprocity, as when women help each other with the many chores of a ceremonial knowing that what goes around comes around so that, when their own girls reach womanhood, there will be many who will help with those and subsequent feasts. The reciprocity principle also operates to keep most people on an even economic basis for, especially in families, when one has, all have. This, however, makes it very difficult for families to save; saving, for its own sake, is not sensible at Mescalero, for one must always share with family. In a way, the Mescalero Apache system of reciprocity is a kind of saving that invests in people rather than in banks.

So with her admonition to, "Go around," Delores inadvertently also lectured, albeit subtly, some of the guests, too, the strangers who did not know the proper way to go around on this Reservation.

Note

[1] As it turned out, Bernard himself sometimes varied the specific colors in the directional sequence. But, in general, darker colors were in the masculine-associated directions and lighter colors were in the feminine-associated directions. This contrast between light and dark *does* hold with other singers and most people, with east and south colors being lighter in hue and saturation than west and north colors. However, the specific direction associated with a particular color is quite variable.

5

"I will give you bow and arrow . . . a flint knife . . . I will make a horse for you . . ."

Ceremonial Day Three

Scuffling feet and the lisping voices of men who had too much to drink awakened me sometime deep in the night. While I was much too sleepy to try to read my watch, it was evident that it was long after midnight, for the drumming and singing for social dancing had stopped and the stars I could see through the smokehole overhead were those of very early morning. Men were walking around our tipi. Just as I was wishing I had Nellie with me instead of having left her and her barking ways at Lauren's, the tipi flap was shoved aside and two forms entered, the first one saying, "Father! Where's the beer?"

"SSSSSSSSSSSSsssssssssssssss!" given in my best Apachean hissing voice. "Go away! There isn't a party in here. There are people trying to sleep in here. Go home!"

Even before I had finished stage-whispering my imperious commands, a man's voice said, "Auntie Ginger [my nickname, from my once-red hair]! Is that you? It's me, Dexter. I didn't mean to wake you. Go to sleep, Auntie. I'll come and get you for breakfast in the morning." Then, to his companion, "Go! Go! She sure gets mad sometimes."

Bernard, who had also been awakened, chuckled and complimented me, "Spoken like a true Apache mother." Our laughter threatened to awaken everyone; so we tried to muffle it, me by putting the pillow over my head and Bernard by burrowing deeper under his elkskin robe.

When I emerged from the tipi a few hours later, my usual sleepy, pre-coffee, self, Dexter was sitting in the ramada sipping coffee and obviously waiting for me. He greeted me formally, "Auntie, you have arrived. It is good to see you again."

The tall, slender, handsome man in front of me bore little resemblance to the skinny, insecure little boy I remembered who had been fostered by Bernard and raised as his son. Dexter was a troubled child who was always into something or another until his single mother and Bernard jointly went to the Tribal Court to have Bernard assume provisional custody of Dexter to try to straighten him out, to give him a missing sense of self-worth, to channel some of his energy, and to enforce discipline that he badly needed. Although Bernard had never formally adopted him and although Dexter continued to remain close to his birth mother, he nonetheless considered Bernard to be his father, making me a de facto auntie.

Instead of replying to his proper greeting in an equally formal manner, I opened my arms and hugged him, commenting upon how tall and handsome he'd become and intentionally avoiding our rather confrontational meeting earlier that morning. But he broached the topic himself.

"As soon as I heard that hiss, I knew it was you, Auntie. And I was instantly sober!" We both laughed as he continued, "I really do want to take you to breakfast. Let's go to the Hilltop and get a whiteman's breakfast with pancakes."

Walking to my car, he told me he now worked as a carpenter, usually in Ruidoso, the Anglo resort community on the east side of the Reservation. He proudly showed me his journeyman's union card and said he had a girlfriend and was thinking seriously of getting married. He then teased that he was sure that she could not cook as well as could I.

"So that's why we are going out for breakfast, right?" I teased back.

Laughing and reminiscing, we drove first to Lauren's; I wanted to shower, wash my hair, get clean clothes, and put on some mud-free shoes. I was also feeling a bit guilty for dumping Nellie at the house so told Dexter we'd have to stop at one of the meadows before going to the restaurant so that I could let Nellie run a bit and give Lauren a respite from dog watching.

At the house there was a clamor from the three children who wanted to accompany us to Ruidoso and a breakfast out; however, they had already eaten by the time I emerged from the shower. I promised I'd take them for ice cream in Ruidoso later in the day, in the afternoon when it was hot. "You mean, *if* it gets hot and doesn't rain again," Jay interrupted.

"No, I mean whether or not it rains and whether or not it is hot. Just you children and I will go into Ruidoso later in the afternoon. OK?"

It really wasn't OK, but they agreed, since it was clear they were not going with us this morning. I asked Lauren what I should pick up at Safeway, besides oranges, before coming back to the house. I'd brought coffee, a ham, lard, and flour with me, but I'd somehow forgotten the oranges that Delores so dearly loves. We did a quick survey of cupboards and refrigerator, devising a list of needed food and supplies. Ruidoso is close, but it is also takes well over an hour from Lauren's house by the time one drives out of the big canyon, through the meadows, past the Inn of the Mountain Gods (built to attract tourists, and very successful as a Tribal enterprise), by the Rio Ruidoso, through the narrow but always busy canyon between the Reservation and Ruidoso, into the town proper, to a store (just try to find a parking space in the summer horse-racing season!), and then back again. No matter the original purpose of a trip into Ruidoso, one does as much business as possible to avoid having to make the trip twice in a day.

As Dexter and I sat down to breakfast, we were immediately and politely served water along with the menu. In normal circumstances, that would not be an exceptional act. However, in Ruidoso it sometimes becomes out of the ordinary. Just a couple of years earlier, Indians were not served water in Ruidoso without surly remarks about having to pay for it or bringing their own. Once, just two years before this breakfast, Harold, Lauren, the children, and I were made to feel so uncomfortable in a Ruidoso establishment that I wanted to leave the restaurant. But Lauren insisted Apaches do not run away from fights and sensibly observed that our money was as good as anyone else's. It was not, however, a pleasant meal, not what we originally intended when we decided to go out for dinner.

Almost all of the water for the town of Ruidoso rises on Apache land. And, while the Tribe has never cut the supply or threatened to do so, it seems to be what Ruidoso residents fear most. A couple of years previously, the Mescalero Tribe had entered litigation with the State of New Mexico over water rights. During the period of the court case, water was a sensitive issue in Ruidoso, accounting for—but not excusing— the dinner waitress's attitude. I was grateful that case was settled and we could order a meal as normal people do without having to be confrontational over something as basic as water.

After our breakfast and errands, I drove Dexter back to the ceremonial grounds, where his truck was parked, before returning to Lauren's. I decided to stay at the house, since it was a quiet day in terms of ceremonial activity. While there is certainly plenty to do on the ceremonial mesa and on the mesa adjacent to it, I am not particularly intrigued by rodeo activities that were to take up most of the afternoon. Also, there is an afternoon powwow, but I have seen countless powwows and couldn't think of a compelling reason to view another one despite the colorful costumes and showy dancing. There was more than enough to do at the house anyway.

Lauren and I did laundry, shampooed the girls' hair, and put on a pot of chili stew that filled the house with a tantalizing fragrance. Jay and Delores quickly became bored with us and went out to look for their horses (there is no corral at Lauren's) while waiting for lunch to be ready. So the house was quiet after we dried Nancy's hair and put her down for a nap, because her cold was still bothering her.

We sat at the dining room table and talked while Lauren did some of her exquisite beaded work (a handsome belt buckle) with small, faceted beads (called "cut beads"), and I applied the yellow powder to a deerskin that would soon be a pair of moccasins. She teased me that I should also "finish" my shoelaces with some color. The previous afternoon I had broken a shoelace in my tennis shoes. Bernard cut two pieces of pure white buckskin for me to use, rather than having to see me appear in public with the knots I'd tied in the broken lace. The new laces were made so I would not "embarrass this whole family looking like that with those sorry shoelaces."

We hadn't been working for very long before a van pulled up in front of the house. Woden, Marilyn, and their two boys, all cousins of Lauren's and Bernard's from Oklahoma, had arrived for the remainder of the ceremonial. They would be setting up their tipi next to ours on the ceremonial grounds.

The sound of the van also brought Jay and Delores back to the house, sans horses. They were probably grazing somewhere further up in the canyon. I put on the cast iron skillet to begin heating lard for fry bread while Lauren and Marilyn deftly patted out the rounds. During ceremonial times, and powwow times too, at Mescalero one always cooks extra food, for friends and relatives come in numbers and at all hours of the day or night. People are always offered food; besides, it was almost two o'clock and time for lunch anyway.

After eating, Woden, who is a very large, commanding man, declared that he and Marilyn were taking Delores with them to the ceremonial grounds. "All the way from Oklahoma with those two boys! We're just sick of boys. We're gonna take this girl with us now."

Delores shivered with delight. She is a special favorite of her Uncle Woden and Aunt Marilyn, as she calls these cousins who are the ages of her own parents. (Woden is from Mescalero; Marilyn is Cheyenne, a highly respected tribe at Mescalero.)

Woden continued, "Get your camp dress and shawl and new moccasins. We're gonna watch you dance at the powwow. And if we don't get you a good partner, I'll dance with you myself."

We all chuckled at the thought of that, for Woden is almost 6'5" tall, and Delores is a slender, short child. She dashed to comply.

A camp-out dress is a two-piece dress fashioned after late 1800s pioneer clothing: an overblouse that fits loosely and has large sleeves, worn over a fully gathered, and sometimes ruffled, long skirt. Delores had a new camp-out dress Lauren had made just for this ceremonial, knowing Delores's love of dancing. The dress was of a lovely dark blue and white calico print. With her long, dark hair, finely chiseled tiny features, and new moccasins to fit her new foot size, she would indeed be a pretty picture of a little girl.

As she was getting her clothes together and stuffing her moccasins into a plastic bag, Jay reminded her that if she went with Woden and Marilyn and their boys, she would miss the trip to Ruidoso. "It's OK, Jay. Auntie always brings ice cream back anyway." True enough. She knows me well.

So, as Delores climbed into the van to go the ceremonial grounds and the powwow, Jay and I got into my car to go into Ruidoso for ice cream. Nancy slept through all the commotion.

As usual, Jay had a hidden agenda and "needed" to stop at a department store "just for a minute, Auntie." His Uncle Woden had given him some money that was burning a very big hole in his pocket. Actually, the department store was on my list of things to do as well, for Lauren had mentioned that Jay was "sure growin'" this summer and would need all new clothes for school and that it wasn't as easy to sew for boys as it was for girls. She would never ask me outright to buy clothes for the children, because my own budget might not allow such expenditures. Nonetheless, her statement made me aware of a need that she'd rather see filled than my buying toys for the children as I usually did. What I actually chose to buy was up to me and would be received with the same gratitude, whether or not it was what she felt he needed.

Jay, of course, headed for the toys. He did not find what he wanted: a small pocketknife. I had one with me that I was going to give him as a going-away present; instead, I told him I had one for him in the car that was supposed to be a surprise, so he could choose something else. He chose a tee shirt depicting a popular cartoon superhero and then put it back, realizing he had enough money only for his own tee shirt; he would have nothing left over for his sisters. A proper brother, he would not buy something only for himself and then flaunt it to his sisters. So we agreed that I would buy small things for his sisters, and he could spend his money on his tee shirt. He carefully chose small toys for each of his sisters and could hardly wait to pay for the tee shirt before donning it. While we were there, I also bought a few items for each of the children for school. Then, it was finally ice-cream time.

Jay chose a cone with two different flavors of ice cream in it, while I chose an ice with marshmallow sauce. We sat inside enjoying our treats and debating the merits of the different flavors, trying to reach a decision about what kind to have packed to take back to the house.

A man came over to our table and greeted Jay, asking him if he was practicing during the summer. Jay looked acutely embarrassed. I introduced myself and the man told me his name, adding that he was the Ruidoso elementary school physical education teacher and Jay was on his soccer team. Since Jay's family lives closer to Ruidoso than they do to the elementary school on the reservation, the children go to school in Ruidoso. But Jay had lied to the coach by saying he was practicing. Even after the man left our table, Jay seemed upset and lost interest in his by-now-dripping ice-cream cone.

"Do you want to tell me about it, Jay?" I queried.

At first he did not answer me; he just looked down at the table. Finally he said, "I lied." I told him that I knew he did, but the man should not have embarrassed him. I said that I knew he lied because the man wanted to hear that he was practicing during the summer, and it seemed Jay did not want to practice nor to discuss soccer—or much of anything else for that matter. But I also said that I did not understand, since I had thought that he liked playing soccer.

"I do! Really, Auntie, I do. I like soccer. An' I'm even good at it."

"Then I don't see the problem, Jay. I don't understand why you are not practicing, if you like it so much. Maybe there is something else. Maybe there is something you should tell me."

Jay looked as though he was going to cry; he was obviously distressed. Even marshmallow sauce that I offered him didn't perk him up at all. Finally, he told me what was bothering him.

During the last game of the school term, the Ruidoso elementary school team was scheduled to play the team from the Reservation elementary school. Probably in an effort to "psych-up" the team, and certainly not thinking of the individuals playing on it, the coach I'd just met had told the boys how good they were, what fine players they were, and how they were going to beat the tar out of those "dirty Indians." Jay looked pained. After a pause, he continued, "I'm Indian, aren't I, Auntie? I'm not dirty."

What do you say? How can you ease a child's ache when that child confronts prejudice? How could I make Jay realize it was a figure of speech that probably his coach didn't really mean?

What if his coach really did mean it? How difficult it must be for Jay to try to learn from and respect such a person. No wonder he had temporarily given up on soccer, no matter how much he loved the game. How could I justify the coach's statement, regardless of the intent? I understood why Jay lied. With me still trying my best to reassure him, we fled back to the safety of the reservation, and I determined I would keep Jay with me for the rest of the day and evening; he needed to feel special.

When we went back to Lauren's, I announced I would be taking Jay with me to the ceremonial grounds. Lauren said she'd see me at the tipi after dinner and see whether Jay would stay with me all night or go back to his own house.

On the ceremonial grounds I gave Jay some money so that he could go to the concession stands while I told Bernard what had happened with the soccer coach the previous spring. Bernard said Indian children had to get used to such statements and learn not to let them bother them. I said that was a lot to ask of a little boy. Bernard did not argue with me but instead said we should be back in the tipi a while before dinner.

I took a camera and went to look for Jay; shooting pictures usually perked him up, and it did this day, too. We sat high in the grandstands while Jay shot pictures of powwow dancing, including his sister, Delores, who really did end up dancing with her Uncle Woden.

After she had danced, we spoke to her to tell her how well she did and how pretty she looked. Jay took a sticky mass out of his pocket: candy he'd bought at the concession stands with the money I'd given him. He had carefully divided it into three parts, using, he assured me, his new knife. One part he'd save until he saw Nancy, but this part was Delores's. She did not seem to mind that it was in less than pristine condition.

Jay told Delores of our shopping and said there were surprises for her and Nancy at the house. "Ice cream, too?" she asked. When Jay responded positively, she said, "I told you Auntie always brings some back." Delores is becoming a woman of the world, I mused.

An hour or so before dinner was to be served, Jay and I went back to the tipi, ostensibly to reload the camera with faster film for the night's dancing of the Mountain Gods that I told him I wanted to photograph. Woden and Marilyn already had their tipi set up next to ours, and Delores sang out to us from inside it as we passed by.

As usual, our tipi was filled with Bernard's friends from around the country, talking and visiting. After I settled down on my mattress and had my camera reloaded and set up for the night's dancing, Bernard told Jay to bring him my tape recorder. Bernard turned it on, and told me to get out my notebook, for he had a story he thought I would want to hear and note down. It was really a story he wanted Jay to hear, but, as we agreed later, there was no sense in not recording it since he was going to be telling it anyway.

> When we first became a people, before . . . before there were human beings on this earth, there was only the Sun and the Mother Earth. Between the union of the two, our two Spirit Warriors came into being and they were our predecessors. From there, mankind came, as we believe.
>
> And in the beginning of time, God said to a people, "This is your land; walk on it; walk on it with respect and, in return, it will give you everything. Do not mistreat it and it will always bring forth what you need."
>
> And we try to remember that in a world of blasphemy and in a world of unbelieving. We remember that.
>
> There is a song that is sung about this mountains when we are far out in the Plains and we see our mountains in a distance, in a haze; we are returning to it; we say, "I remember. I remember the blue mountains of my country—with lonesomeness. As I approach it, I am— happiness fills my heart, for it is everything to me: it is my food pack; it is my sun shade; it is my home."
>
> Mother Earth came to us as White Painted Woman. She told us of her own children, of the Warrior Twins. They said, one said, "Oh, my mother, I have come forth to you. What will you give me?"
>
> "I will give you bow and arrow and I will give you a flint knife. Go forth and be a man. I will make a woman for you, that you will propagate. I will make a horse for you; I will make a horse for you, that you will be a horse people and that he will be your brother. Live in a good way, a holy way, in a world of kindness and of dignity."
>
> Some races have forgotten that.

And, I noted to myself, some coaches may never have learned it.

The mythic present joins narratives from long ago with situations from the contemporary world. More than family stories, these culturally shared narratives not only speak to proper behavior of self and fellows but also are used to comment upon improper behavior of outsiders. The ignorance, and sometimes hurtful nature in comments like those of the coach, can be placed in a context that allows both retention of one's own self-esteem while not belittling another.

To have forgotten, as Bernard characterized the coach and his people, is more charitable than my thought that the information had never been learned or perseverated. Thus, the mythic present also allows one to maintain dignity in the face of prejudice. And, perhaps as importantly, invocation of the mythic present in such instances simultaneously defuses the situation and provides a context that allows life to continue without the need for retaliatory action to save face.

6

"You are the mother of a people. Let no man speak ill of you."

Ceremonial Day Four

This is the most important day of the ceremonial, according to Bernard. It is the day when The People once again assume their proper responsibilities vis-à-vis the appropriate running of the world.

Throughout the previous nights of the girls' puberty ceremonial activities, the singers have recounted tribal history. On the first night, they sing the songs of The First Grandfather, the Grandfather of the East. Metaphorically this means that they sing of the first day of creation and of subsequent events associated with that first day of bringing into being. Similarly, on the second and third nights, they sing songs dedicated to The Second and Third Grandfathers, those associated respectively with the South and West. These songs not only recount what occurred on those second and third days of the initial creative burst, but also they relate what happened in subsequent epochs that are associated with symbolic events of the second and third days. On the fourth night—that does not end until the full disk of the sun clears East Mountain on what Anglos perceive to be the fifth morning[1]—on that fourth night, the songs concern The Fourth Grandfather and the North as well as relating subsequent events that brought ^{n}dé to their present place of residence. Even more importantly, during the last few songs sung before sunrise, the singers implore The People once again to assume the burdens associated with the proper unfolding and on-goingness of the word as we know it.

In the few moments immediately before full sunrise, at the end of the fourth day (Apache reckoning) or beginning of the fifth day (Anglo reckoning), there is an important ceremonial blessing of the girls. This blessing time, called Pulling the Sun, must be preceded by careful planning. At the beginning of the fourth night, the singers are constantly alert to what is happening in the night sky. By watching the stars transit between the poles of the ceremonial tipi and by watching the positional movements of nahakus/the Big Dipper, the singers are able to time their songs and the girls' ritual activities so that all will be ready for Pulling the Sun at full sunrise. This means that the singers begin their timing at about 8:00 P.M. and do not finish it until shortly after 7:00 A.M. of the following morning.[2] But before the sun can be pulled, there is much ceremonial activity that occurs.

As on the other nights, the girls are led into the ceremonial tipi on the last night by their singers. Each takes her/his own place. When all is in readiness, the head singer begins shaking his deer hoof rattle, setting the tempo of the songs. The girls rise to dance on the cowhide mats spread in front of them. As the girls dance, the singers relate matters that occurred on the last day of creation, matters associated with symbols brought into being on that last day of activity by Creator, matters that occurred as the Apachean (and Navajo) people were migrating ever southward from their original home in the northwestern parts of Canada. They sing, as well, of what happened to the tribe as a whole in recent times. And, before each head singer retires from his duties, he may, if he so chooses, add a song of what occurred to the tribe during his own term as head singer.

During all of the singing, the girls dance. And during all of the singing, I, in those years I was present, took my place immediately behind Bernard's folding chair, holding his hat while listening to the songs and watching the girls dancing. On this last night, the songs go on and on, for there is much that must be related. Two breaks are called, usually around ten o'clock and at about midnight, so that the girls can rest. Then, somewhere between half past one and three in the morning, the last of the ceremonial tipi songs is sung, and the girls retire to their camp-out homes for other rituals that must be performed before the sun is pulled.

In the camp-out areas, the girls' ceremonial dresses are removed by their godmothers and mothers, who also bathe them and wash their hair in yucca root suds. Next they dress the girls and put their ceremonial clothes on them again. And then they are painted so they may appear as living reincarnations of White Painted Woman. Singers or godmothers use a white clay mixture to paint the girls' legs and thighs, their arms, the backs of their hands, their shoulders, and, finally, their faces. The stark white paint does indeed transform them, as they appear to be almost other-worldly beings.

In this form, as the living representative of the mythological White Painted Woman, the girls are led into the ceremonial tipi for the final time. As the singers finish their face painting of the girls, they turn to painting their own palms with symbols of the sun. Already the sky is beginning to lighten. Both singers and girls sit on the ground now, facing the east. Men move about the open east end of the ceremonial arena, making sure no one crosses the opening and keeping it clear of spectators.

Soon a soft singing is heard from the singers. With each of the four sun-pulling songs, the singers move their hands into different positions until, finally, as the last verse of the last song is sung, they extend their arms over their heads, with their palms, the sun symbols painted on them, open and facing toward the sun. Then, if the timing has been proper, just as the last note of the last morning song is sung, the sun tops the mountains to strike the men's upraised palms. Their hands provide shade for their own faces and for the girls sitting behind them, but not before a flash of newly risen sunlight fully illuminates the inside of the tipi and the girls arrayed around its inner perimeter.

Quickly, men begin to deconstruct the ceremonial tipi,

On the last morning, just before the full disk of the sun clears the eastern mountains, Bernard Second paints a sun symbol on his left palm. (Claire R. Farrer photo.)

leaving only the tetrapod of The Four Grandfathers standing. The tipi is de-constructed in reverse order as it was constructed: last pieces on are first pieces off. The interwoven boughs are pulled off the bottom of the tipi, so that the entire assembled crowd can see the girls as they represent White Painted Woman.

In a ritual reminiscent of the first day's blessings, each of the singers paints the face of the girl for whom he has sung. Some paint red and white circles or crosses, some paint yellow and white crescents. Then the singers also paint the faces of all who are in the long lines, awaiting blessings from both singers and girls. Once again, those with particular complaints linger a moment to have the afflicted parts of their bodies especially blessed.

Again, in a ritual reminiscent of the first day, the girls are lined up after the blessings have been completed. But on this last day, they stand in a south-north line, facing east, while the head singer, or one of his assistants, paints four perfect, crescent, pollen moons on a pure white deerskin. As the pollen filters through the singer's fingers in a tiny but continuous stream, he prays for a long and fruitful life for each of the girls/women whose public presentation is almost completed. He prays them through the segments of their life courses, bringing to a formal close both their infancy and childhood while moving them firmly into adulthood.

When the painting is completed, the girl for whom the head singer sings is moved onto the white deerskin. Her left foot is placed on the first of the crescent moons, and a song is sung about infancy. Next her right foot moves forward to the second crescent while the singers sing a song associated with childhood. Then, her left foot steps on the third crescent, and a song for adulthood is sung. Finally, her right foot moves onto the fourth crescent, and a song celebrating old age is sung. Quickly, her singer and godmother push her off the deerskin and she begins the first of her four concluding runs to the east. Rapidly, the girls/women standing in line with her step lightly on each of the four crescents and join her in her run. As on the first day, they circle a basket four times. However, on this last day, the basket is moved farther and farther from the ceremonial tipi; this symbolic statement is that, although the parents long to hold onto their daughters, they realize that their girls are now women, moving into the adulthood stage of their lives.

On the fourth run around the basket, that now is a considerable distance to the east from the ceremonial arena grounds, the girls again circle the basket four times. Instead of returning to the ceremonial tipi after the four-time circling of the basket on the fourth and final run, the girls run toward their camp-out homes, all the while rubbing the paint off their faces. They are met by female relatives who guide them to their camp-out homes.

Most people, however, do not see them running to their camp-out homes for, as soon as they complete the four turns around the basket on their final run, the Four Grandfathers come crashing to the earth. This literally bone-rattling event causes people to turn immediately to the source of the noise. By the time they have turned around again to look for the girls returning from the east, the new women are gone. When next they are seen, it is as Apache adults, no longer resembling White Painted Woman physically, but each about to embark on her role as the mother of a people.

Again, in an echo of the first day, pickup trucks pull up in front, on the arena side of the cooking arbor, and again goodies are thrown to the assembled crowd. Meanwhile, one of the most moving of the entire ritual activities occurs in the privacy of the camp-out home.

Ever since the parents of a girl have decided to have their girl go through a ceremony, that girl has been subject to the instructions of the man who will sing for her. He tells her to be chaste, not to be seen alone around boys, not to cut her hair, to behave only in certain rather rigid ways, to be careful of what she thinks and says, to be kind and respectful especially to all those older than is she, to be generous—to display all the positive aspects of proper Apachean womanhood. During the course of her ceremonial, he is even more strict with her: she must not stare or even look most people directly in the eyes; she must maintain a proper demeanor at all times; she must dance whenever he sings; she must always be accompanied by at least one other person no matter where she is or what she is doing; she must bless the food all are to eat; and on and on. Then, at the conclusion of her last run, when she is once again safely nestled in her camp-out home, while she is contemplating all she has been through, once again he confronts her.

But this time, he comes to her as a supplicant. He kneels in front of her and takes her left hand to cradle inside his outstretched hands. He reminds her of all she has endured, of all he has demanded of her, of all she has accomplished, of how well people speak of her. He recites her genealogy to her, recalling her ancestors on both her mother's and father's sides, telling her she comes from a proud and intelligent line, a proud and successful people.

This year, to Stephanie, while on his knees before her, Bernard said, "Never forget, my daughter, you bear a *proud* name. Geronimo *led* his people; he sacrificed for them. Much of what we have today is because of him . . . Let me hear your name spoken only in pride. Never let me hear any man speak of you in disrespect. This is a good thing you have done these four days. Never forget it. You are from a *good* family, a family of pride, generosity, and respect. You are a good woman. Never forget that, my daughter." He hugged her and continued, "I will always love you, my daughter."

Then, three times he placed small bits of food in her mouth, telling her both of her importance as a nurturer and of the proper foods of The People. He reminded her she is now a woman and, as such, has power even exceeding his, for now, as he said, "You are the mother of a people. Let no man speak ill of you." He kissed her and left to bless the food that was soon to be shared with all awaiting breakfast, while her godmother placed a fourth morsel of food in her mouth, symbolizing her being fed by all the women, of all time, of her tribe.

Invariably, all present during the singer's final speech to his ritual and ceremonial "daughter" are moved to tears. While the new young woman looks as serene as a Michelangelo madonna, the observers (parents of the girl, close family members, and perhaps a select friend or two) find tears streaming down their faces. Truly, now they are in the presence of a new Apache woman.

Often, the new young woman relates having had a mystical experience, either during the previous night when she danced all night long, or during the morning's painting of her as White Painted Woman, or during the last of the four runs. Sometimes the women report seeing the path their lives must follow; sometimes they realize the vocation they must pursue; sometimes they understand religious mysteries; sometimes they experience events that must later be interpreted for them by singers or medicine people. Almost invariably, the girls report having been changed, not only into social women but also at a very basic level. They are ready to put aside their childhoods and become full adults of their tribe and community.

In the old days, many of the girls would marry immediately upon conclusion of their ceremonials. Now, however, they must first finish school and, for many, there is also college to be completed before they marry and start a family, before they actually become the "mothers of a people."

Notes

[1] Again there is the issue of time. Apaches reckon days from the time when the full disk of the sun clears the horizon. Anglos reckon days from midnight. So there is a minimum difference of five hours between when a new day

begins for Anglos and Apaches. Apaches experience little conflict between the two systems. But Anglos often cannot come to terms with the differences; this is especially true during the ceremonial when a day that Anglos perceive began the previous midnight is believed, by Apaches, not to have occurred at all. This happens if anything—fog, rain, an overcast sky—occludes the sun and keeps people from seeing the sun's full disk clear the horizon. Such Anglo days are considered to be a part of the previous day by Apaches, since a new day cannot begin until the full disk of the sun is visible above the horizon. Sometimes the disjunction is particularly difficult for Anglos to comprehend when the Apache people go back to work on such a day, only to return on the next day that the sun is visible to continue the ceremonial. The canceled day in Anglo terms is simply regular time and not ceremonial time to Apaches.

[2] Recall that the reservation is mountainous and, therefore, apparent sunrise is usually later than astronomically derived sunrise.

7

Going Home

While the ceremonial girls seem energized by their experience, the singers, by contrast, are exhausted. Most go directly home and sleep—sometimes around the clock. Especially during the summer, when there are many ceremonials in addition to the public one held over the Fourth of July holiday, singers are in demand and seem to be in almost constant sleep deficit. This year, as I brought some of Bernard's things to his house from the ceremonial campground, I found him sleeping soundly, with his house doors open, fully clothed, even to his boots. I covered him and quietly closed the door as I left.

For those of us who are spectators, there is also an emotional coming-down time. I don't think there is anything much lonelier than an empty tipi and campground after almost everyone is gone. What a sense of solitude it is, especially after living in such close proximity for almost a week. How horrible the banishment punishment must have been in times past, when the most serious of infractions resulted in the perpetrator being permanently expelled from the tribe. Even if encountered again, such miscreants were ignored as though they were not present; no one spoke to them or acknowledged their presence. It was as though they were transparent. When one grows up in a closely knit family among relatives and tribal members, being forever alone is harrowing.

For four days and four nights, and more than that for many people, we have lived as an aggregate group, sharing meals, sharing rituals, sharing sharing, and reestablishing bonds that languish during the rest of the year. Now, suddenly, camps must be struck. The pillows, mats, mattresses, tables, chairs, coolers, clothing, towels, pots and pans, and even the tipis themselves need to be carried back home. Our family always tries to strike all of the tipis and other camp-out structures at once, as a group. We laugh and joke with one another and often share a final meal together either at someone's home or at a restaurant. It eases the pain of living separately once again after our week or so of intensive communal living.

Camp-striking time is always a time when I wish the ceremonial were just a few days longer. In some years, I can afford to stay on for a while. But in other years, I must return to teaching or writing. It is difficult to be alone after sharing everything for a brief week; Nellie is great company but she does not talk much. So usually I try to stay on for at least a few days, if not a week or two. There are always things to work on: new stories to be told; more language to learn; more time to spend intensively with children; new skills to learn from the women; more stars to watch and learn about, especially those that are important to the Apache people; books and book chapters to be discussed and corrected.

Later that week, after Bernard has slept the clock around and then some, I learned that Hilda and Sol had given him a white buckskin shirt, a black shawl, an Appaloosa mare registered on both sides, a beautifully tanned buckskin, a Pendleton blanket, food, money, and tobacco for singing for their daughter. Bernard considered it generous payment. He kept the shirt, the mare, some of the money and food, and the tobacco; and he redistributed the rest to others. (Even that which he kept he shared with his family.)

Bernard and I had been working especially with astronomy that year, and there were some loose ends he wanted to tie up before I left. Since I had finally become competent in understanding basketry design, he wanted me to move on and understand more about the stars as clocks.

The indoctrination into basketry design had, at first, seemed to me to be an interruption in Bernard's teaching me about the stars. However, since Mescalero Apache basketry is famous and highly prized among collectors, it was a diversion I welcomed. When finally I understood and could name the basketry designs, it was also apparent how they are tied to the sky and to the Long Ago, even if made in the lived present.

Recall that Creator in only four days made the world as people know it today. And recall that there are four stages of life through which we each pass, if we have a normal life span allotted to us. As the previous chapters demonstrated, the girls' puberty ceremonial lasts for four days; this is a reminder of the four days of creation. The four stages of life also harken back to creation. But the four stages of life are also a reminder of White Painted Woman. Again, the mythic present is important in the lived present. And, obviously, four is an important number for Mescalero Apache people.

Similarly, basketry indexes the mythic present while replicating aspects of important narratives in a visual mode. Properly made baskets, as distinguished from those made on commission for a tourist, are constructed in fours or in multiples of fours. They are said to be in balance and harmony when the designs on them can be divided into fours, so that one-fourth of the design, when replicated, produces the design seen on the entire basket; they are quadrilaterally symmetrical. And they are almost always round.

The roundness of basketry reproduces the roundness of the universe, as perceived by Apaches. They say that any fool can tell the world is round just by looking at the sky. Each day the sun comes up in the east and moves through the south before setting in the west. Since it will again rise in the east, it makes logical sense that it passes through the north during the night. Not only does this account for the quartered circle of the pollen blessings, but also it accounts for the knowledge that the natural universe exists in the round.

There are other examples of roundness in the sky as well. People who go outside at night to observe the stars very quickly note that the stars seem to move around a pivot point that, in the Northern Hemisphere, is called the north pole or sometimes the North Star. The stars and constellations close to the North Star are called circumpolar, since they are visible all year round, making their tight circles around the North Star.

But there is more to observe as well. When we watch the stars throughout a year, it becomes apparent that they move

Figure 5. This "star" design basket shows the typical divisions into fours that characterize Mescalero Apache baskets. (Drawn by James R. Yingst from a Claire R. Farrer photo of basket #48103/12 of the Laboratory of Anthropology of the Museum of New Mexico, Santa Fe, New Mexico.)

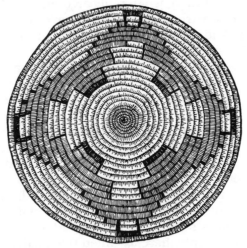

Figure 6. The "Four Stages of Life" design is considered to be a particularly pleasing aesthetic depiction, by Apache people. (Drawn by James R. Yingst from a Claire R. Farrer photo of basket #36736/12 of the Laboratory of Anthropology of the Museum of New Mexico, Santa Fe, New Mexico.)

seasonally, too. At sunset, the constellations become visible. A constellation that appears on the eastern horizon shortly after sunset in September, for instance, will be in another quadrant of the sky three months later. From these regular nightly, seasonal, and yearly movements, star watchers quickly become aware of the year's natural division into four parts. Once again, Apaches aver, the importance of four is paramount.

So it is no wonder that designs on baskets also are in fours. Perhaps it is more accurate to state that a design is repeated four times on properly made baskets.

The closeness between baskets and the sky is further enhanced by the design names. What Western-trained people usually see as four, linked, petal-shaped outlines, each taking up one-quarter of a basket, Apache people see as sųųs/star. Whenever Apache people draw stars on paper, or stitch them in colorful beads onto clothing, their stars are of four points.

Another four-part design that is common is called shaʔ/sun. This design is of a central circle with four design elements at right angles to each other, forming what Westerners see as a cross on top of a circle. However, the Apache sun design has extensions at the ends of each of the cross pieces; the extensions are said to be the rays of the sun as it shines. Indeed, when people look at the sun, it is so bright that it does seem to have lines streaming from it. (Don't try this! It is easy to burn the macula of one's eyes by looking directly into the sun, and burning out the macula means blindness!)

Other designs are named for other sky phenomena or items from narrative. What they all share in common is that they are in fours or multiples of four.

After having taught me the relationship between the sky and design, especially that on basketry, Bernard continued my education by teaching me how the stars can be used as clocks.

The stars he uses to time events throughout the ceremonial shift seasonally. This year he actually used planets and their relationship to the backdrop of the stars, since there were bright planets in good positions in the south-southwest. He began this year's timing by first sighting Saturn along the side of the East Grandfather pole; he then looked to the south-southwest and watched the movement of the stars in relationship to Saturn. (See the sight lines marked on Figure 4 on page 60.)

"First look just south of East Grandfather," he told me. Then he related how, about an hour and a half later, he looked to "a little star" between the poles around South Grandfather. Shortly after 10:00 P.M., Anglo time, he began using nahakus, followed around 3:30 A.M. by Three-In-a-Row (or, The-Three-Who-Went-Together) and Morning Star. While watching the star clock, he paid attention to both angles and positions in relation to the horizon. He stated, "Occasionally we might have a ceremony in the wintertime. Then it [the star clock] changes; it's different . . . it all changes," but there are always stars to watch. Even as the sky apparently shifts through the seasons of the year, there is always the Big Dipper. There are always stars in the south-southwest. And there is always a Morning Star.

He continued,

> Then on the last day, in the morning, we look directly to the east, then the Morning Star comes up . . . and I have to keep watching it until it gets at a certain distance above the mountain ridge; then is when they quit [in the ceremonial tipi] to start ending [prior to hair and body washing of the girls] whereas on the Plains it would be different . . . I'm always outside at night an' I'm always looking up so I know the changes with the seasons. Even in the wintertime I get up and walk around outside at night and watch them so I'm familiar with it, 'cause of the seasonal changes . . . It's still the same except for the seasonal change; you have to remember that it's changed . . . We always look at the Dipper no matter what season . . . I don't know how to explain it. We know because, ah, I just *know* it. I can gauge by it . . . whether it's in December or July, I can gauge . . .
>
> Star-That-Does-Not-Move and the Morning Star are also constant. . . . dependable, we always see them. As long as we see them, it doesn't matter what angle they're at. When we see them, we guide ourselves by them. . . . In the mountains there are certain peaks where they hit . . . Whereas on the Plains, it's different. But then, even then, say when I'm in Oklahoma . . . there's nothing around . . . I can still tell. You just know.

"You just know." It seemed so simple to Bernard but so difficult for me, who had spent most of her life indoors and who seldom looked at the sky. His teaching me about the sky was

Nahakus, the Big Dipper, is an important constellation used both to tell the time of night and the season of the year. Here the dipper indicates about 10:30 P.M., Mountain Daylight Time, in mid-summer. The handle stars of the dipper are on the right side of the tipi poles while the bowl stars are above the light pole. (Gene Ammarell photo.)

very complicated: partly because it is considered to be primarily men's knowledge at Mescalero, and I am a woman; partly because I was so ignorant of my own culture's notions of the sky that I had little background from which to draw for baseline knowledge or for comparisons; partly because I could spend so little time at Mescalero and so did not have many nights outside with Bernard; and partly because the system of measurement is so different.

When a person looks up at the sky in the Western world, that person usually has a star chart in hand that shows the major constellations and that has instructions for how to orient oneself by looking in a particular direction at a specific time. When a person looks up at the sky at Mescalero, there is no guide—only a vast canopy of colored lights. (The stars are not all white lights in a dark sky, as most Western people assume.)

Bernard began teaching me about the night sky by asking me to awaken him at a particular time of the night or very early morning. We would then go outside, and he would ask me what time it was. Being a rather slow learner, I (for longer than I care to admit) rummaged around in my backpack for my flashlight that I would then shine on my watch before answering him. His inevitable response was, "Pay attention!" That, of course, made me grumpy, for there I was outside in the cold when I wanted to be sleeping and then being chastized on top of it all! But finally I realized he meant that if I would pay attention to the sky, I would not need a watch.

With that marvelous discovery, I thought our sessions would go more quickly. I was wrong. As Bernard would try to point out a particular star to me, he would use a lip gesture and say something like, "*That* [lip gesture made by using the muscles of the lower lip to form it into a V, then raising his chin and 'pointing' in an area that seemed to me to take in at least 20° and a prodigious number of stars] blue-green one, two handspans up."

And I would get frustrated all over again. "Two handspans up from what?" I often asked, none too politely. If there was a convenient landmark—perhaps a tree or a large boulder or maybe even a mountain—in the line of sight, he would then mention it. Then I would want to know, "Your handspans or mine?" It was Bernard's turn to be frustrated with me, after such questions.

It turned out to be simple, although I never would have bet

on it in the beginning. A person stands facing a horizon and extends her arms out in front of her at shoulder height with palms facing the ground. Then she rotates her wrists and raises her arms slightly so that her palms are moved to a 90° angle to her arms; this position results in her palms facing her eyes. Next she raises the bottom of one hand, say the left one, until it appears to rest on the horizon. She tucks her thumb into her palm. What she then sees over her four fingers is one handspan up from the horizon (or about 10°). By placing her right hand, again with thumb tucked in, on top of the left one, she can view two handspans up (or about 20° above the horizon). Simple!

But that was only the beginning. To be a competent star watcher at Mescalero requires years of watching until the sky becomes as familiar as the back of one's own hand. Skillful star watchers, and there are very few of them now, can look at the sky and quickly determine their position in space as well as how far they are from known landmarks. With such knowledge, timing a girls' puberty ceremonial using only the sky becomes a relatively easy exercise.

How much of this knowledge will remain? I wondered. In order to know the sky as intimately as did Bernard, one needs to be able to walk around at night throughout not just one year but many of them. The celestial vault is vast with stars beyond comprehension. Learning which of them are significant and which are useful for the purposes of ᵑdé takes years of dedicated watching. Those years cannot be devoted to the night sky when there are state laws mandating that children must be in school for most of the year. A child cannot walk around all night with an uncle to learn the night sky and then also be alert in school the next day. What will happen to star knowledge?

My dream is to open a planetarium in the southwestern part of the United States, a planetarium devoted to Native American astronomy. It will be a place where people such as Bernard can bring children to teach them the importance of the things in the sky. And it will be a place where, through the projector and the dome, Native American experts on the sky can present their views to a larger public than has even been possible.

Dreams are important. Just before I leave, I listen to the dreams of the children.

When Jay was a tiny boy, he used to say that he would be a singer himself when he grew up. But, despite years of trying, he could never stay awake all through the night. Now he says that maybe he'll dance as a Mountain God when he is bigger. Perhaps he will, or perhaps he will return to his original plan. Adults will not push him one way or another; it is up to each individual to decide what path should be followed. Parents might be disappointed with a choice or feel that another is more appropriate, but ultimately, Mescalero Apaches believe that no individual, not even a parent, is wise enough to choose the path another should follow, not even for one's own child.

Delores says, as she plays Nintendo in front of the big-screen television, that she will have a ceremony when she is old enough. She usually accompanies me in the ceremonial tipi, often falling asleep for a nap in my arms or at my feet, wrapped in my jacket or in that of her uncle. She already knows how to do the dance steps the ceremonial girls do—both of the steps. She already knows how she must behave and refuses to allow her hair to be cut, so that it will be properly long when she has her ceremonial, even while decorating it with the latest in hair-ties or barrettes that Indian and non-Indian children alike adore.

Nancy is still too young to make her decisions, but she has a tendency to follow her adored older sister. She plays with her Barbies or Cabbage Patch dolls while telling me how she helped her mother skin the elk and how "its insides" look to one just learning how to butcher and dress meat.[1] Her dreams, while not yet fully formed, already combine both the Anglo and Indian worlds.

Whatever the girls choose, their brother, Jay, will be there to support them and to assist them in whichever ways he can. A short while ago, Jay decided he would come to California to live with me. He did not change his mind, despite the pleadings of his mother that he wait until he got a little older. His resolve weakened only as he and I were poring over the map, and I was showing him the places where we would stay overnight on our drive back to California. "You mean, Auntie, that I can't come back here on weekends?"

"That's right, Jay. I guess I can put you on the bus or plane so you can come back to the reservation at Thanksgiving, and we can both come back at Christmas. But between the time school starts and Thanksgiving, you cannot go home. It would take you three days, if we drive."

He looked so saddened as he dropped the Teenaged Mutant

Ninja Turtle toy he was fingering onto the pile of Smurfs and GI Joes. With one of the bigger sighs I have ever heard from a child, he said to me, "I can't go to California with you, Auntie. You're just gonna have to live alone. I can't leave these little girls here. They need their brother."

And so they do, more than I need a little boy to live with me and keep me company. Boys and men are essential to the well-being of families. Brothers and sisters form a lifelong bond; they help each other, and they take care of each other throughout their lives. During a girl's puberty ceremony, a brother is important to his sister as he shields her from the sun at appropriate times, brings her things she cannot get for herself, entertains her, carries water for her, helps construct and deconstruct her ceremonial tipi if he is big enough, encourages her when she is tired, and in general is there to support her in whatever ways she needs. As they both mature, he will make sure her children have enough to eat and enough to wear. He will become the disciplinarian of his nieces and nephews while their biological fathers become their confidants and adored friends.

A proper brother cannot abandon his sisters for the pleasures of being an only child in California. Who would take up their cause? Who would speak for them when others spoke slander? Who would see to it that they had their proper share of everything? Who would ensure that there was ice cream and candy, as well as meat and potatoes, for all? A brother is an important person in any sister's life. Being three days' drive away is simply too far, especially for a little boy who already feels keenly his responsibilities toward his sisters.

So instead we talk on the telephone, Jay and I, and the other children as well, although it is usually Jay who initiates the contact. He lets me know that he is also a proper boy toward the ascending generation, toward his Auntie who is so poor she lives alone, without a child in her house, without her relatives close to her (a situation almost unthinkable to him). Although the distances are great, Jay tends to me almost as carefully as he tends his sisters. As he says, "What are little boys for?"

We both know the answer. They are for taking care of the women of the family, whether it is bringing them coffee (and remembering who likes how much sugar or cream) or telling them how pretty they are in their powwow dresses or helping them raise the children or in bringing older aunties their shawls as the fat begins to shift under their skin and they easily take a chill. Boys and men take care of the mothers, all the mothers in their families—even those who have never borne children and who perhaps never will.[2]

Maybe Jay will become a singer after all. Maybe it is acceptable as a little boy, a very young brother, to fall asleep during the nights' singing. Maybe little boys need that sleep for the times later in their lives when they will become the watchers while the mothers of a people sleep.

Notes

[1] Lauren tells me that she had to reassure Nancy continually during the butchering of the elk that Lauren had received from one of her nephews, who had shot it. Nancy assumed, from the size and general contours of the animal, that it was one of the horses; and she was reluctant even to look at it, let alone help butcher it. Lauren says she had to round up all the horses and let Nancy see for herself that they were all there before Nancy would help. It later developed that Nancy, who had seen elk only from a distance, thought they were the size of large dogs. When her parents learned that, they made sure that she saw a live elk up close. She was reassured and is now proud of beginning to learn how to butcher meat.

[2] In a matrilineage there are "classificatory mothers." These are the sisters and female first couisins (through one's mother) of one's mother. They, too, are considered to be one's mothers, even if they have not given birth.

8

A Personal Epilogue

In June 1990 I stopped in Chicago on my way home from almost six months living and teaching in Ghent, Belgium. The stopover had two purposes: to ease my jet lag, which I do not handle well under the very best of circumstances, and, with Tom Curtin of Waveland Press, to negotiate and sign the contract that eventuated in this book. I had, six months previously, completed a scholarly book on the Mescalero and, along with the active encouragement of the management of Waveland Press, wanted to do a book for a more general audience. The book was already outlined, but there was no proper ending. No matter; the contract was signed.

Now, in May 1993, the book is finished, and is much overdue—largely because it still had no proper ending. First, let me tell you about one of the beginnings and then I shall come back to this business of ending.

When I returned to my permanent home in California, I had a very hard time with reverse culture shock. The term "culture shock" is what anthropologists call the often difficult process of adjusting to a culture that is not one's own: smells are different as are housing, food, ways of interacting—the list continues on and on. Personally, I have always felt it more difficult to return home than to go out into the field—whether the field is an Indian Reservation or an ancient city in Belgium. On the way out, there is the anticipation of the wonderful new things to be encountered. On the way home, I always miss things I have left behind that I wish I could make a part of my life in my "real" home.

Ghent, Belgium is only a few kilometers from the North Sea and the English Channel. Usually it is humid and cool. My part of California is often hot, hot, hot, hot. And I think that surely June 1990 must have been one of the hotter Junes, or so it seemed to me and my body recently attuned to a milder climate. While eager to begin working on this book, it was just too hot and my mind had not yet caught up with my body—to say nothing of my body readjusting to a time zone nine hours behind the one in which I had so recently been living while I was in Belgium.

In order to increase my comfort level by escaping a bit from the heat of June and to keep up the amount of walking I had become accustomed to while living in Belgium, I determined I would go to an air-conditioned mall a couple of times a week and walk the perimeter. Although I soon tired of it, the first day I went contributed directly to this book.

On the day of my first mall walk after returning from Belgium and while I was still firmly in the throes of reverse culture shock, I found an unexpected arts and crafts exhibit and sale in the center of the mall. It was comforting to see the specialty booths and stalls for, among other things, I missed keenly my daily purchase of freshly baked bread accompanied by "Goedemorgen, professor doktor." I had become used to specialty markets or at least specialty stalls, often outdoors, and was a bit overwhelmed by all the stores under one roof and just the general vastness of it all. Yet, I was delighted, too, since I enjoy giving hand made items for family gifts; so I extended my walk a bit and shopped the booths.

One booth in particular caught my attention. A tiny, old, Oriental man, who is unknown to me by name and is represented only by his signature, in Chinese characters, and a chop mark—neither of which I can read—was making and selling exquisite brush and ink drawings. I bought some for presents and, as I was reaching for money to pay for them, he said to me, "When you spend over $30, you get one free. Which one do you want?"

I looked through all of the paintings before saying, "I don't want any of these. The one I want isn't here. I want just one, plain, horse." At the time, I am embarrassed to say, I didn't think how terribly rude and brusque I was being.

Kindly ignoring my rudeness and appalling lack of manners, the gentleman produced a long, rectangular piece of paper and in less than five minutes handed me what you see as the cover of this book. He said, "Here. He was just frightened by thunder."

I was literally stunned speechless: a very rare, if not unique, occurrence, my friends maintain. This man I had never met before (and have not seen since), from where I did not know, had seemingly read my very thoughts and made me precisely the right horse. I could not have done as good a job describing what I wanted as he did by intuitively making precisely what was in my mind's eye. The "Thunder Horse," as I think of it, is not only on the cover of this book, it also hung on the wall behind my word processor as I wrote. Indeed, it hangs there still.

Occurrences such as the magical Thunder Horse coming to me are commonplace occurrences on the Mescalero Apache Indian Reservation, where they are integrated into the belief and behavior system with no difficulty. It is simply another example of the mythic present. Those same occurrences are a different matter in rational, Western-based cultures. Usually, it is easier for me to handle such experiences when I am on the Mescalero Apache Indian Reservation myself, for they are not considered extraordinary there but rather are considered gifts from That One Which Sustains The World and The Universe. I was properly thankful for my gift and placed it on the wall where the Thunder Horse seems ready to burst from the frame and gallop through my study, indeed the entire house, in a frenzy of massed energy. He kept me writing in those times when I could get into the study and away from grading papers or preparing lectures. And, on those days when the writing was going particularly slowly, I liked to think that perhaps some of his explosive energy would find its way onto the pages of the book taking shape on the word processor.

But still I had no ending for the book, although the exquisite Thunder Horse gave me a fine beginning. I fervently hoped the ending would materialize before the writing was completed. It didn't.

Chico, California, where I teach at California State

University, is a community with a large variety of restaurants and is also a vital art center for Northern California. Both are combined in Cory's, one of my two favorite lunch places. Cory, the owner, not only serves delicious home-made food and sinful desserts, but also she makes the walls of her restaurant available to local artists. Each month the exhibit changes. About a year after returning from Belgium, beginning this book, and having the Thunder Horse magically appear, there was a stunning Native American art exhibit in Cory's. One of the featured artists was Kicking Horse Edward Buie, a part-Sioux man who was then working on his master's. And among Kicking Horse's works was the end-piece of this book, what he calls "Thunder Being" and what I think of as the Lightning Horse.

Kicking Horse's Thunder Being (my Lightning Horse) is a blue-grey war horse, arrayed with a shield, feathers, a saddle blanket, a bow, arrows, and painted zig-zags. The zig-zags are in the same form that Mescalero Apaches use to represent lightning. Further, those zig-zags are red, a color usually assigned masculine properties at Mescalero, and fully appropriate for the Warrior Twin who rides the blue horse of Lightning in one version of the narrative of creation.

Again, shaking my head at the gift of just what was needed, I bought a print from Kicking Horse and secured his permission to use it in this book. But the walls of my study were already filled, so Kicking Horse's horse reposed in a closet awaiting shipment to Chicago to become a part of this book.

Chapter 7 was completed. All the earlier chapters were finished. The book was ready to go. But it wasn't. I still felt there was no proper ending. Ending with dreams and the uncertain future of a little boy I dearly love certainly seemed poetic but a little unreal, as well. The Mescalero Apache people are not a dream people. They are real, alive, vital, and struggling to maintain themselves and their identity in a world not of their making. So I tried writing things of that sort, but they all fell flat on the page, ending with a thud rather than with a bang or at least a question.

Hoping inspiration for a dynamite ending would hit as my old Imagewriter printer laboriously spun out page after page, I began looking for a suitable box in which to place the printed manuscript as well as both magical pieces of Thunder Horse and Lightning Horse. As I rummaged around amidst boxes and packing material, the phone rang. I placed Lightning Horse between the printer and computer so it wouldn't fall and dent its mat while I talked on the telephone.

Finishing the conversation, I went back into the study to measure the two pieces of art for their shipping box. Suddenly, it was obvious that Lightning Horse was the ending I sought—indeed, I'd had it for a long time and did not realize it.

Note that Kicking Horse's Thunder Being, my Lightning Horse, is not only the proper color for the Lightning brother of the Warrior Twins and not only has what I perceive as lightning on his head, neck, shoulders, flank, and legs, but also he is pinioned. He is a carousel horse—forever elegantly dressed and forever going nowhere. He is an apt visual metaphor for contemporary reservations, such as that at Mescalero.

What contemporary Native Americans face is precisely the accommodation that Thunder Being/Lightning Horse represents. There is value in tradition; it is to be celebrated and even displayed on occasion. But today's Native Americans must fight to stay afloat, surrounded as they are by the vastly larger mainstream American culture that pinions them every bit as much as if they were themselves positioned on a carousel.

Self-determination, a goal of every Native person I know, is not a reality on Native American reservations. Each reservation Indian is subject to a whole panoply of federal laws that take precedence over Native customary law. Indian people must also deal with laws of counties and laws of states. Crimes (such as rape, murder, and other offenses) that can be tried in local and state courts throughout the United States are federal crimes on Indian reservations. Pinioned.

Polygyny can no longer be practiced by Native Americans; it is illegal in the United States. Pinioned.

When Native people take advantage of their federal status, as with opening gaming places on their reservations, there is a great outcry from local people, especially politicians who covet the lost tax revenues, since, by federal law, reservations are tax-exempt. Pinioned.

When special, valued resources have been discovered on Native lands, those lands have been subject to outright takeover by the United States government. Even when the Bureau of Indian Affairs, the federally mandated trust agent for Indians, manages the lands or acts as trustee for the tribe, there is often corruption in the form of graft or 'forgotten' payments. In order to rectify these issues, Native people must spend long years in the courts. Pinioned.

The Warrior Twins are still revered at Mescalero. Thunder still rides his black horse; Lightning still rides his blue horse. But, as Thunder roars and Lightning strikes the ground, they are chained to it: pinioned. It is almost as though even the Warrior Twins astride their magical horses also had carousel poles through them. The mythic present is still important, but it is constrained by laws and actions of the federal government in lived reality. Meanwhile, the lived reality is that of confinement, broken promises, broken treaties, and enforced dependency. Is this really the ending?

The tension represented by the Thunder Horse of the cover and the Lightning Horse at the end of this book mirrors the tension in contemporary Indian America. This is a tension that has torn families and reservations apart. Yet, I am a person of enormous hope; I am not one to predict the downfall of the Native American. Nonetheless, I worry about the pinioning, the enforced adherence to situations not of their making and the lack of true self-determination on contemporary reservations.

But, as I think of the people I have grown to know and respect on the Mescalero Apache Indian Reservation, I am confident that they will find ways through the tension. I know that the mythic present and the lived present are together strong enough to one day break the bonds represented by the pinioned carousel horse.

When that day comes, Thunder Horse will turn his head northward, whinny a call to his newly freed brother, and together the two horses and their Warrior Twin riders will lead The People into the destiny promised them in prophecy—no longer pinioned, no longer elegant but on display, no longer confined, but vital, eager, proud, and free.

Glossary

au	yes
bizaaye	little, small amount
dibéhé	sheep
dii	here
ʔehųkaʔuʔitu	offering black bittersweet water; coffee
gish	cane
gutąął	one who sings; a singer (of ceremonies)
ʔIsdzanatłʔeesh	White Painted Woman (Sometimes also called Changing Woman. Mother of the Warrior Twins.)
koʔio	go around; circle around
kughą	home (Refers to a "proper" home—that is, a tipi.)
lizhi	black (the color)
Mescalero	people of the mescal (Comes from Spanish; mescal is the root of the giant agave, or the century plant. It is a carbyhydrate source, not an hallucinogen.)
nahakus	The Big Dipper constellation
ⁿdé	The People (that is, Mescalero Apaches)
nełįįyé	dog; literally burden bearer (in the old language)
shaʔ	sun
shilaa-n	my sibling (Without the "-n," it means my hand.)
shimá	my mother
sųųs	star
tadidiin	pollen (especially of the cattail tules)

tainashka?da	three who went together (This is understood as being three people who either traveled together and/or died at the same time.)
tiswin	corn beer
wickiup	a domed-shaped arbor (Usually constructed of saplings bent to form a frame with boughs interwoven as walls and roof; oak is the preferred material.)

References

Farrer, Claire R.
  1991 *Living Life's Circle: Mescalero Apache Cosmovision.*
        Albuquerque: University of New Mexico Press.
Hall, Edward T.
  1967 *The Silent Language.* Greenwich, CT: Fawcett
        Premier.
  1969 *The Hidden Dimension.* Garden City, NY:
        Doubleday-Anchor Press.
  1977 *Beyond Culture.* Garden City, NY: Doubleday-
        Anchor Press.
  1983 *The Dance of Life: The Other Dimension of Time.*
        Garden City, NY: Doubleday-Anchor Press.
Williamson, Ray A.
  1987 *Living the Sky: The Cosmos of the American Indian.*
        Norman: University of Oklahoma Press.
Williamson, Ray A. and Claire R. Farrer
  1992 "Introduction: The Animating Breath." In *Earth and
        Sky: Visions of the Cosmos in Native American
        Folklore.* Ray A. Williamson and Claire R. Farrer, eds.
        Albuquerque: University of New Mexico Press, pp.
        1–24.

Study Guide

prepared by
Daniel E. Moerman
University of Michigan, Dearborn

These questions and comments are designed to help you think about *Thunder Rides a Black Horse* now that you have finished reading it. They are based on my thoughts about the book. As I read it, I thought about what Farrer was saying, and about what I wanted my students to see in the book. I tried to think about how different readers might react to the book— male, female; black, white; younger, older; immigrant, native-born—and to see how their different perspectives might be mirrored, or reversed, or transformed by the text. To that end, I enlisted the aid of my graduate research assistant, Tina Palivos.

These questions ask you to take different perspectives yourself, to try to imagine life from a perspective different from your own. To do that, you must be aware of the perspective with which you begin. Much of the value of an anthropological perspective—examining an "other" lies in how it forces us to see ourselves. As is so often the case in American anthropological writing (and most other American writing for that matter), this book has an implied audience that is, by and large, white, middle class and male. Those of you who are not white, middle-class males will be able to learn about two different sets of cultural expectations if you observe both the object and the audience here. Those of you who *are* white, middle-class males (like me), will have to work a little harder to see that.

115

The point of reading this book is not to learn the facts. It makes a substantial difference that the book is about Apaches (not Navajos or Iroquois), that they live in the southwestern desert (not a rainforest or a Polynesian island), that they have a matrilineal system (rather than a patrilineal or a bilateral one). You won't gain much of value from the book if you don't notice and remember these sorts of things and incorporate them into your understanding. Indeed, among the most important things you might learn from reading this book is that there is no such thing as a "fact" unmediated by an interpretation based on a set of categories and understandings—in some part what Farrer calls the "mythic present" that, I think, is always part of everyone's life.

Pages 1–3:

Farrer says that "reality" is an "oscillating movement between the mythic present and the lived present." The mythic present is what "happened long ago," but which is also real and present during everyday life. Real experience involves *interaction* of the present and the past. The past involves memory of personal experiences and memory of stories told of other experiences by other people and interpretations of those memories. Why does she go through this? What is the point? Isn't "reality" obvious?

Reservation life is different from modern life not because of the difference in the "every day" (they have TV, 4 x 4s, Wonder Bread, Power Rangers), but because it has a different past— Warrior Twins, sweat lodges, buckskin, frybread. And so, the Apaches' *present* is different than ours; their past will be different than ours; therefore, their future will be different than ours. What do you think about this?

Farrer implies that mainstream Americans live only in the present. What do you think about this? Can George Washington's purported actions in regard to the cherry tree be a part of mainstream America's mythic present?

Pages 3–5:

Time. Apache dances begin only when all the dancers are ready and dressed, the musicians are assembled with their instruments, the events announced—not necessarily at 8:00.

This, she says, irritates Anglos, who live by monochronic time rather than polychronic time.

If you are an Anglo, think about her argument. When does someone decide to get married? To have children? To go out to the movies? When does the rock band decide to start playing? What is going on here (because you *know* that you get irritated when the dance doesn't start at 8:00!).

If you are neither an Apache nor an Anglo, what kind of time do you use? When do events occur? Why do they occur *then* rather than earlier or later? What kind of conflict might develop if that sense of time came in contact with Anglo time? With Indian time?

It may be possible to say that Anglo time focuses more on the needs of *observers* of events, while Indian time focuses more on the needs of *participants* in events. What do you think about this?

Page 6:

"Most Native North American people live simultaneously in two cultures"—they are enriched by having two traditions to draw on, but often feel impoverished by not being fully accepted by either. Have you ever experienced anything like this? Have you traveled away from home—maybe while you were in the Army or the Peace Corps, or as an immigrant, or as a visitor to the land from which your family emigrated? Sometimes the contrast Farrer describes occurs in a family across generations—when a farm family moves to a city; when an auto worker father has a son who is a lawyer, or a daughter who is a doctor; or when the child of a wealthy businessman plays in a garage band. Describe an experience you have had (or might have, or someone you know has had) like this. Why are such experiences hard? What can we learn from them about human life? About the mythic present?

Passim:

This question is for women only. Throughout the book, the author refers to her daughter, Suzanne, who spent much time on the reservation with her mother from the time she was about twelve years old. Try to figure out Suzanne's story. At one point, she arranged to be adopted by an Apache family so she wouldn't have to leave the reservation. Why did she do this? Can you tell from the book? Suppose that when you were twelve your parents forced you to leave your friends, your home, your school, and went to live on a dusty reservation in New Mexico where girls have puberty ceremonies. What would you do? What do you think about this?

Pages 10–11:

What do the photos of Second and Farrer suggest about long-term fieldwork? Is it reasonable for a consultant to write fieldnotes for the anthropologist?

Page 13, Footnote 1:

What is a "month"? Do some research on this. Find several different ways that people divide up the year. What is the relationship between lived experience and the mythic present in a concept like a month? Have you ever had any lived experience regarding months?

Page 15:

Psychologists tell us smell is the most evocative sense. What smells mean home to you?

Page 16:

All cultures—and many ethnic groups within cultures—have creation narratives. Which narratives are "true" in your life?

Pages 20–24:

Lauren refers to The-Three-Who-Went-Together as she tells the author what has happened to an old woman with Alzheimer's disease. Farrer tells us that a long story lies behind Lauren's brief mention of The-Three. Can you find an example like this from your life? Are Apaches different from Anglos in doing this? Why don't we notice these sorts of things in our own conversation? Do you think Lauren noticed it in hers? Why do anthropologists go to far away places to talk with fictive sisters about old women who have Alzheimer's disease? Farrer writes that since Lauren mentioned the story while they were eating, "generosity is quickly indexed." What does she mean by the word "indexed"? Why is it that generosity is indexed rather than something else, like recipes or table settings?

In the story about The-Three-Who-Went-Together, much happens. Consider these:

a. "The more they shared, the more they had to share." How is this possible? Why does the author leave $20 on top of the refrigerator, rather than handing it to her sister? What is "reciprocity"?

b. The Shaman visits "The Real World of Creator and Power from This World of Shadows and Illusions." What is the relationship here between reality and illusion? The three people end up as three stars in the sky. What is going on here? Did this really happen?

c. In this family, two sisters are married to the same man. In some Islamic countries, men can marry several women at once. What do you think about that? Anglo women are allowed to have two, three or six husbands, but only one at a time since polygamy is illegal in the United States. Why? What does it mean to say that polygamy is right or wrong?

Page 27:

Why do anthropologists believe they have been accepted into their fieldwork culture when they are teased or can participate in jokes? What does it take to make or understand a joke? Is it acceptable to joke with everyone in your society?

Pages 30–32:

Delores is corrected by Bernard, her mother's brother. Farrer says it is proper for Delores' uncle to correct her, but not proper for her father, Harold, to do so. Why is this?

Page 32:

Sometimes it is difficult to understand the kinship practices of another's culture. Using the symbols on page 32, draw your own kinship chart, beginning with your grandparents. Then put a check mark [✔] in the symbols for those who are your matrilineal relatives. What happens?

Pages 35–39:

Bernard tells the author a story about the beginningtime, about the origins of rain and of Thunder and Lightning ("Thunder rode on a black horse"). Farrer says, "Apaches *know* that calling Rain's ritual name in narrative [in a story] results in calling the physical presence of rain to oneself" (note 5; italics added). After Bernard told the story, it started raining. What does it mean to "know" something? What would have happened if it hadn't rained?

Page 41:

Why does Bernard address Claire in both Apache and English? Why might it be important for an anthropologist to learn the people's language of her/his field site?

How can Farrer claim not to hear what is happening around her? Are there times in your life when you do not hear what happens in a room, a class, outside?

Page 44:

The caption of the photograph on page 44 says "St. Joseph's Catholic Mission Church can be seen in the background." Why do you think the reservation has a mission rather than a parish? See what you can find out about missions on Indian reservations.

Pages 46–53:

Farrer explains that an Apache girl becomes a physiological woman when she has her first menses. This experience is celebrated with the girls' puberty ceremony that helps the girl become a social woman. What marks the transition from childhood to becoming a woman in your culture? Compare this to the puberty ceremony held for Apache girls. For women reading this, what do you remember of your first menstruation? For men, what do you know and think about women's menstruation? Think about American cultural attitudes toward this transition in a woman's life. How does this reflect the position of women in each culture?

Pages 49–50:

The symbolic meaning of each element of the puberty ceremony is described in great detail. What do you think about symbols? Why do people use symbols? What symbols are important to you?

Pages 52–53:

Transmission of knowledge: throughout the book, stories of the past are told to teach lessons of proper behavior to children in the present (see pp. 52, 69, and 81). How are children taught lessons in your culture? How do you acquire knowledge? Who teaches you about the past? What past do you learn about?

Pages 57–58:

Music and dance: Farrer describes the symbolic and functional elements of the music and dances performed in the puberty ceremony. For example, she says that the Mountain Gods "dance to heal and bless" and "the songs refer to the first four days of Creation." What rituals or ceremonies can you think of when music is used to represent or accomplish something? When do you listen to music? When do you dance?

Also on page 57, Farrer again mentions the turned-up toe moccasin as a marker of ethnicity. What markers are used among your friends, your parents' friends, members of social clubs?

Page 64:

Farrer explains that "at Mescalero an adult is responsible for her/his own behavior; the responsibility does not lie with one's background (deprived or privileged), family, spouse, friends, or any other outside influence." What do you think about this?

Page 65:

"Maybe you'd like some coffee while you do that," is a polite way to ask a question at Mescalero. Do you ever ask questions without using interrogatives such as who, what, how, why?

Pages 68–106:

Colors: among the Apache at Mescalero, colors carry symbolic meaning that connect directionality, gender, space, and nature. For example, Farrer explains that "dark colors are thought to be stronger and masculine, and light colors are thought to be closely associated with femininity." Do you consider some colors more masculine or feminine? What other meanings do you attach to colors? Why do you think colors have meaning?

Page 70:

"The base metaphor, for the Mescalero Apache, includes circularity and sunwise directionality, balance and harmony, patterned sound and silence, as well as the number 4." Throughout the book, these elements repeatedly come up in the descriptions and explanations of Apache origins, rituals, music, art, and everyday life activities. Do you think metaphors influence the way we see the world? Or do you think they are a reflection of our perceptions? Try to come up with some common metaphors that may be taken for granted in your culture. One example in American culture is "time is money."

Page 74:

Greeting and leave-taking speech is formalized among most people in the world. How do you greet others? What rituals do you use on greeting? On parting? Can you do a ritual (such as a handshake) without accompanying speech?

Page 79:

What is a lie? Is it ever considered appropriate to lie in your culture?

Page 81:

Origin myth. Consider the origin story told by Bernard. What origin myth were you taught as a child? How did you learn it? Do you think it has influenced the way you see and understand the world? What do you think about this Apache creation story? How would you explain the differences between two or more origin stories?

Bernard told this story to Jay to teach him a lesson about prejudice. What do you think about race? How did you learn these ideas? Think about the images that you were raised with (e.g., from parents, media, school, friends, and so on).

Page 85:

White Painted Woman is a cultural heroine. Do mainstream Americans have a cultural heroine? What is the difference between a role model and a cultural heroine?

Page 93:

Farrer explains that Apache "basketry indexes the mythic present while replicating aspects of important narratives in a visual mode." She goes on to illustrate how Western-trained people will see the designs differently than Apache people. This illustrates the earlier point that different histories will be reflected in different perceptions of the present. How do you think your past has influenced the way you see and understand things you experience in the present?

Page 96:

Bernard's narrative is very different from those on pages 81, 69, or 52. Why might this be so? What are the differences among formal speech, narrative, and speech to impart conversational information?

Page 101:

What is a "proper brother" in terms of how you were raised?

Page 103:

Culture shock. "The term 'culture shock' is what anthropologists call the often difficult process of adjusting to a culture that is not one's own: smells are different as are housing, food, ways of interacting—the list continues on and on." Have you ever experienced culture shock when traveling away from your home? Why do you think this happens? What does this tell us about the influence of culture on human beings?

Page 105:

"Occurrences such as the magical Thunder Horse coming to me are commonplace occurrences on the Mescalero Apache Indian Reservation, where they are integrated into the belief and behavior system with no difficulty. It is simply another example of the mythic present. Those same occurrences are a different matter in rational, Western-based culture." What do you think of this? How do people think about these kinds of occurrences in Western cultures? Why do they think differently about them than the Apache? What do you think about these experiences?

Page 110:

What did Farrer leave out? What else could have been included to help you better understand Mescalero Apache people? What would you have to include if you were to write about your own people, your own culture, an important event in your culture?